Lily

By

Ronna M. Bacon

ISBN 978-1-998821-33-4

Deuteronomy 31:6 Be strong and of a good courage, fear not, nor be afraid of them: for the LORD your God, he it is that does go with you; he will not fail you, nor forsake you.

Psalm 18:30. As for God, His way is perfect; The word of the Lord is proven; He is a shield to all who trust in Him.

Table of Contents

Chapter 1

Fog hung heavy over the streets and buildings in the town of Elmton. Visibility was severely restricted, down to mere feet. There were few vehicles on the streets, their lights shining dimly through the fog. The dampness that ensued seemed to soak through the jackets of the emergency personnel who had been called to a crime scene not that long before. The fog was hampering their investigation.

Lily Gordon, a detective on the police force, tugged her jacket closer around her body and pulled the cap that she had on her dark brown curls down further over her brown eyes. She didn't want to be there. She hated working out in the fog. She could handle any other weather but fog was too spooky and disturbing. She always envisioned a murder scene in old London, England, when they had fog like this.

"What do we have?" She approached one of the patrol officers, who was standing nearby.

"A murder, Lily." Tim looked around. "And this weather is not helping us preserve any evidence."

"No, it's not. Let's see what we have. Joe's here?" Joe Whyte was the local coroner.

"He is." Tim motioned through the fog. "He's with the body. An older male. A lot of blood around him, Lily." Tim grimaced at that. He hated blood but it was part of his job to handle that.

"There is? Okay. I can't see him. Show me where he is." Lily followed Tim, almost reaching out a hand to grab at the back of his jacket. She stopped abruptly when he did, peering around him at Joe. "Joe?"

"Lily? You won the draw tonight?" Joe gave a quick grin before he sobered. "It's a mess, Lily, and not just from the murder. There is a lot of debris and garbage that your team will have to bag."

"What can you tell me?" Lily stood nearby, her notebook and pen out. She frowned up at the fog, knowing that it would make it almost impossible for her to make notes. She sighed and tucked away the pad and pen, reaching instead for her phone and its note taking application.

"Not a lot right now. He's been stabbed multiple times." Joe paused. "It's like overkill, Lily. Someone hated him and hated him badly." He nodded towards the building where Lily could see faint forms. "The man who found him is over there. He's not saying much."

"I see." Lily continued to make her notes before she stared around the area. Joe had been correct when he told her that there was a lot of debris. It would make the investigation that much more difficult as they had no idea what was pertinent to the investigation or not.

Lily walked towards the building, a hand out to wipe off her face. The fog was soaking her and she hated that feeling. Her eyes took in the man seated on the cement steps to the building. His head was buried in his hands. Lily frowned. He seemed familiar but she wasn't sure that she knew him.

"Excuse me, sir. I'm Detective Lily Gordon. I understand that you found the body?" Lily paused in front of him, her frown deepening.

The man stiffened before his head raised. He squinted at Lily, his hazel eyes studying her. His black hair was cut just long enough to be normal but it was a little bit longer than usual.

"Lily? Is that you?" Loch Longfort had been a friend of Lily's back in their school days. They had lost contact when they had headed off to different colleges

"Loch? Loch Longfort? It's you?" Lily was dumbfounded for a moment, studying the man in front of her before she shared a look with Tim. "We need to talk, Loch, about what you found." She pointed behind her to where she could hear Joe's voice speaking with someone, his voice muffled by the fog.

"It's me, Lily." Loch shuddered as he remembered the scene that he had stumbled upon. He lived in the apartment above the store in the building where he sat. He had moved back to this town to open up a photography store and studio, wanting to be nearer to his friends.

"Talk to me, Loch. What happened?" Lily's brows lowered as the man in front of her hesitated to speak. Tim had walked away at that point, responding to a call from Joe.

"I don't know what happened. I live upstairs in this building. I had parked in my usual spot and then was walking towards the door. I hesitated because of all the garbage that was on the ground. That's not normal for here. I wasn't really watching where I was going and tripped. When I sat up, I saw the man. I felt for a pulse and couldn't find one. That's when I called it in. The officers made me move and sit here to wait for the investigator. That's you." Loch squinted up at her. "I didn't know that you were a police officer. I wouldn't have thought that you would become a police officer."

"It was my dream since I was a child. I just didn't tell anyone." Lily looked discomforted for a moment. "You live here?" She looked up at the second floor, seeing soft lights on. "By yourself?"

"I've never married, Lily. I leave lights on when I go out in the evening. After having friends killed by people waiting in their dark home, I can't not leave lights on when I go out." Loch was on his feet. "I don't know that I can tell you anything more."

A sudden sound had Lily shifting on her feet, a hand reaching for her weapon. She couldn't see anything in the fog. She turned in a circle, sensing danger but not seeing anything.

Loch moved towards her, standing as close to her as he could. He too searched through the fog, feeling the danger as it moved towards them. A soft sound caught his ear and he spun to face that way. Loch's frown deepened as he heard soft movement but couldn't see anything.

Lily had continued to turn in a circle, coming to a stop as she faced Loch's back. Her mouth opened to speak as Loch's body jolted and then he fell backwards into her. The weight of his body took her violently to the ground. Her head thudded on the pavement and she lost consciousness.

Loch's body landed hard, partly trapping Lily on the ground. He didn't move. A reddening stain on his chest spread around the knife that protruded. He groaned as his body shifted before he lay still. There were no sounds in the fog.

Lily raised her head at last, wiping at the moisture on her face. She couldn't understand why she was on the ground or what the heavy weight was that held her there. She shoved at the weight, hearing a groan. Lily wriggled out from under the body, spinning on her knees as she reached for her weapon. Her hand dropped away from it as Tim appeared.

Tim gave a shout for help even as his hand reached to aid Lily to her feet before he was on his knees beside Loch. His hand reached for Loch's pulse, grateful that Loch was alive. A hand touched the knife even as his other hand reached for his radio and called for help.

Lily was on her knees on Loch's other side, horror briefly crossing her face. How had this happened? She hadn't heard anything. Loch had just fallen into her and taken her to the pavement. She felt a hand on her arm, pulling her to her feet and to one side as Joe dropped beside Loch. He had heard Tim's frantic call for help and was on the move towards them.

"Lily? What happened? Who did this?" Tim's hand on her arm kept her still.

"I don't know, Tim. I was talking with Loch and then the next thing I know? We're on the ground. I didn't see anyone or hear anything other than a faint noise." She swayed on her feet, a hand going to the back of her head. Her cap had been knocked off as she fell. She took it with thanks as it was handed to her.

Tim nodded. With the fog that still lay heavy in the air and stifled any sound, it was no wonder that Lily hadn't heard anything. His hand steered her around the gathering personnel to the waiting paramedic rig. He helped her up and then turned as he heard the sound of wheels on the pavement. His hands reached to help raise the stretcher into the back, watching as one of the paramedics jumped up and then he slammed the door behind him. The paramedic rig took off, the sound of its siren muffled in the fog, the lights barely visible.

Andrew McBeth, police chief for Elmton, paced the Emergency Room waiting room. He had been roused by a call from dispatch and had immediately headed for the hospital. He frowned at his watch. The paramedic rig should have been there and wasn't. This was not how it should be. He turned as he heard hurrying footsteps heading his way. Tim appeared, distress on his face.

"Tim?"

"The rig's disappeared, Andrew. They don't know where it is. We found the paramedic who was driving but he's not talking. He's in really rough shape. They're transporting him now but they're not sure if he will make it or not."

Andrew's face whitened at that. He immediately ran for his car, heading for that scene. One of his detectives, a paramedic, and a witness were missing.

This had never happened under his watch. Now they had to find them. Tim was at his side, leaving his car in the parking lot.

"Lily's was okay, I think. The witness, Loch Longfort, had been knifed. I don't know who or why." Tim's voice had the emotions that he was trying to control.

"I understand, Tim. It's not your fault." Andrew stopped at the scene and was out of his vehicle, approaching the resounding officers. The lead officer looked around, his head shaking at Andrew's unspoken question, his own emotions on his face. They had three people missing and a well-liked paramedic who may well die. And they had no clues as to who or why.

God was in control, Andrew knew, even as he began to pray for all involved. He had no doubt of that. He just wanted his friend, Lily, back and safe.

Chapter 2

Lead detective Bill Buckley unlocked his office door and reached for the light switch. He squinted in the bright light before setting his travel coffee mug on his desk and dropping his briefcase beside it. He yawned before he glanced at his watch. It was only five in the morning, early for him to be there. Bill had reached for his cell phone when it chimed, rising rapidly, dressing and then heading for the office.

Bill had been up and down over the night. His young son, Michael, had been restless and not willing to settle down and sleep. Bill had elected to be the parent who rose in the night, even though he was due at work the next morning. His wife, Cora, was expecting their second child and he had wanted her to get as much sleep as she could. Cora had protested but simply smiled as Bill had kissed her and then sent her off to bed.

Turning as he heard footsteps approaching his door, Bill frowned at the detective who stood there. Jason Long was a good friend of his outside of their duties and apparently had been called in as well. He looked around him for Lily, knowing that Lily had been the one on duty overnight.

"Where's Lily?" Jason's words echoed his thoughts.

"I have no idea. I just got in." Bill yawned once more. "I thought that she would be here. Where's Andrew?"

"I heard that he's on a crime scene but would be in shortly. I don't like this, Bill." Jason frowned at his friend.

"I don't either." Bill was out of his office and heading for Lily's. The door was locked. "She should be here. We all got the call to come in and to come in stat."

"I know." Jason turned as he heard footsteps. "Andrew?"

"Bill. Jason. We need to meet with the others. Head for the conference room." Andrew walked past them, a stoop to his shoulders. He knew that his wife, Phoebe, would be praying for them. He glanced at his watch. It was early but he knew that their minister, Silas, would be open to coming in and meeting with the officers. He was their chaplain and had done that many times before.

"Silas? It's Andrew. I'm sorry to wake you up. We need your chaplain services this morning." He could hear Silas moving around.

"I'm on my way. What can you tell me?"

"Lily is missing as is an injured person. The paramedic rig that they were in is gone as is one of the paramedics. The paramedic who was driving is in critical condition. We don't know if he'll make it." Andrew drew in a deep breath, his emotions mixed as he spoke.

"I'll be there in five. I'm praying for you." Silas walked quietly from the house, leaving Madigan and their young daughter sleeping. He would catch up with her later.

Bill approached Andrew. They were good friends and he could see that Andrew was distraught, to put it mildly.

"Andrew? You don't call us in like this without reason."

"No, I don't. I was called about three hours ago. Lily was at a crime scene and was injured in a mild manner, I think. The man who she was interviewing was stabbed. Tim said they couldn't see anything for the fog. While they were being transported to the hospital, the rig was stopped. The driver is in life-threatening condition. The rig has disappeared. We don't know where they are or who took them."

Bill stared at him in shock. This had not been what he had expected Andrew to say. He immediately began to pray for Lily and whoever was with her.

Andrew turned as he heard his name called out. He reached for the paper, a frown on his face as he did so.

"We have two other people missing. A general surgeon and an anesthetist. They were taken as they walked out of the hospital." Andrew continued to frown.

"They took them, whoever has Lily. They want them to work on the man who was hurt. How was he hurt?"

"He was stabbed in the chest. Joe was on scene working the murder that Lily was investigating."

Andrew pointed towards the conference room, nodding at Silas as he disappeared into the room.

"The chest? That's why. They want him for something and don't want him dying on them." Bill was worried and frustrated. Lily had become a good friend of his and Cora's. She was a Christian, he knew, and trusted God to protect her. He just didn't know what danger she was actually in. He walked into the conference room and found a seat at the back of the room.

Andrew walked to the front of the room and nodded at Silas. Silas stood and began to pray, his voice filling the silence in the room. He stood for a moment before he walked to the back of the room and chose a seat beside Bill.

Andrew searched the faces of the men and women in the room. Word had gotten out about the situation. He sighed to himself. This is not what he or the officers or civilian employees needed. They had been through enough with what he and Bill had faced when they were in the midst of their adventures.

"People, word had spread, I know. Lily is missing. The witness that she was interviewing was stabbed. When he fell, he took Lily down with him. They were being transported to the hospital when the paramedic rig was stopped. The driver is in life-threatening condition in hospital. The rig with Lily, the witness, and the other paramedic has disappeared." He paused as he heard murmurs around the room. "I was informed not too long ago that a surgeon and an anesthetist were abducted from the hospital parking lot. Our assumption is that they were taken to work on the witness. We can't confirm that of course. We need to work on finding Lily and the others. The supervisors will work on sorting out who works on that and who will continue with the normal routine. We do not set aside anything routine but be aware of where you are and be alert for any information that may come your way."

Silas was on his feet again, heading towards Andrew. An arm around Andrew's shoulders kept him in place. Silas stared at the faces staring back at him.

"I know not all of you are believers. That's fine. It's your choice. But I know and am confident that God is in control. He will be there in your investigations. The church prayer chain will be activated as of now as will the ones from the other churches. If any of you need to be prayed with or just to talk, find us. We will be available for that at any time of the day or night."

Bill was on his feet and headed for his office, Jason at his side. He stared at Jason who stared back. They didn't know where to start their investigation but they would start it where it all began.

Chapter 3

Bill walked the alleyway outside of Loch's building. He was puzzled. He had talked to Tim and to Joe. Neither of those men could explain what had happened. They had not seen the assailant, the fog had been too thick. Bill turned to stare at the two-story building. He had learned that Loch lived on the second floor and used the first floor for a studio. He shook his head but was no further ahead in his investigation.

Jason walked his way, having done his own search. There was nothing now to show that a murder had taken place or that an assault had as well. They both knew that the people on the street would be working to help them out. It's what their town did.

"Bill? Anything?" Jason paused beside Bill.

"Not a thing. I did talk to one of the crime scene techs who worked the scene. They took everything, including every bit of garbage. They didn't know what would be important." Bill looked around. "I don't see any sign of anything."

"And there should be." Jason was frustrated. "How do we find them?"

"Prayer, Jason. We've seen that work many times in the past, both for Andrew and me and for our other friends, including your sister."

"We have." Jason's sister, Julia, had been targeted by human traffickers and it was only God's grace that had saved her.

“It’s just so bizarre. Why stab him and then kidnap him?” Bill was trying to think that through. “It doesn’t make any sense.”

“No, it doesn’t. Longfort is a photographer.” Jason looked around before he walked to the front of the store and tried the door. The door opened under his hand. His shout had Bill running that way. “The door’s open, Bill. I doubt that it should be.”

“I doubt it.” Bill’s weapon was in his hands as he entered the shop, the words “Elmton Police” called out as they searched the store and then headed up the stairs to the apartment. Once again the door opened under Bill’s hand this time. He shared a look with Jason before they searched the apartment. The look of the apartment was not what they had expected to find.

Jason’s phone was out as he called it in. Loch’s apartment had been searched and searched rapidly. Whoever had done that deed had not cared that he had left a mess behind him.

Bill watched as the team worked away before he walked down the stairs and outside. He studied the building, not seeing any security cameras on it. He studied the buildings around it, seeing Jason walking his way.

“Jason?”

“I asked about security cameras. With the fog, nothing was picked up. That’s about what I expected.” Jason was frustrated at that.

“It is about what we expected. They’re not picking up much either.” Bill pointed back towards the building. He walked back to his car and slid inside, his finger tapping at the steering wheel. He then drove away, heading for the hospital.

After parking in one of the spots reserved for emergency vehicles, Bill walked towards the hospital. He prayed that he would find information there that would help find Lily and the others. He didn't think that would work. He also needed to find the surgeon and the anesthetist. Bill was deeply worried about them. His thoughts were that they had been taken to treat Loch. He just didn't see why.

Finding one of the security officers, Bill followed him to the security office. He thanked the man and then turned to the officer in the room.

"I need to see the security feed from early this morning." Bill didn't have to say anything more. The officer knew what Bill was looking for.

Watching the feed, Bill saw the two physicians exiting the hospital, seeming deep in conversation. He frowned as he tried to see through the fog for when they disappeared. That didn't happen. The fog was too deep for him to follow them much past ten feet or so from the door. Bill was frustrated, to say the least, that he could not find any more information. He took the thumb drive with the video clip on it and tucked it into an evidence bag which he in turn tucked into a jacket pocket.

Andrew looked up from his desk work as Bill sank into the chair in front of his desk. He pondered his work as he looked down at it and then looked at

Bill. Sitting back in his chair, he waited for Bill to speak.

"I couldn't see anyone who took the two physicians. The fog was too heavy. I have the video clip but it's not helpful in finding out who took them." Bill's frustration came through loud and clear.

"I see." Andrew was thinking through what they knew. "I understand that Don is still in surgery." Don was the paramedic who had been stabbed and left for dead.

"That's what I'm told. I'll head back over there in a while to see what the situation is." Bill sat for a moment. "Longfort's building was broken into and his apartment trashed."

"It was? You're working it?"

"Jason is. I headed for the hospital instead." Bill stared at Andrew. "What is going on?"

"That we don't know as yet. I suspect it will take a while to determine what is really going on. It's Lily that I'm worried about." Andrew very seldom spoke his thoughts like that.

"Me too. And Todd. And then there's Loch Longfort. What do you know about him?"

"Nothing. What have you determined?"

"He's a photographer, well known from what I can tell. He's from this town." Bill had not been surprised to determine that but he did want to know where he had been over the last twelve years. And he would find out, one way or another.

Chapter 4

Jason walked back through the department, shuffling through the paperwork that he held in his hands. He was puzzled by the break-in. Nothing seemed to have been taken or nothing left. He couldn't be sure until Loch had gone through everything but who knew when that would happen. Jason paused to pray for his friend and the others who had been kidnapped. He turned as he heard a voice beside him.

"Jason?" Bill watched him closely, a frown on his face. "What did you find?"

"Not a lot. The team took fingerprints but we need Longfort's to compare. They suspect that whoever it was wore gloves. We can't tell if anything is missing without him going through it. I'm working on tracking down family in town." Jason paused, rubbing at his cheek. "What do we know about him?"

"Not a lot. Look into him. I'm working the physician angle. Not that I have much information on that." Bill was frustrated and it was obvious.

"No word on them?" Jason watched Bill as he shook his head. "Why take them? Other than the obvious, that they were needed to treat someone."

"I just pray that it wasn't Lily. It could have been for Longfort. Not that it helps if it was for him. We have no idea where they are."

"I would think a larger building. If they tucked the paramedic rig inside, we would never find it. How's the paramedic?"

"He was in surgery. I need to go back later and see if he's awake enough to speak with. I'm not holding out hope that he will be." Bill walked away, a slight slump to his shoulders that wasn't normal.

Jason turned to his office, dropping into his chair. He scrolled through his text messages and then listened to his voice mails. He reached for the folders that lined his desk and began to work, stopping every once in while to stare across the room, lost in thought.

Bill headed for the downtown area of Elmton. He hesitated for a moment before he headed into a diner and sat, nodding at the server as she held up the coffee pot. He waited patiently for someone to appear. It was now late afternoon and Bill would head home soon. He just didn't want to, feeling as if he was letting Lily down by doing so.

The street person watched Bill before he walked by the table and just dropped a dirty piece of paper on the tabletop. Bill's hand went out and quickly retrieved it to drop into his pocket. He was on his feet, money dropped to the table to pay for his coffee and then walking rapidly to his car. He sighed. Bill prayed that this would tell him where Lily was. Opening the piece of paper, he frowned. This was not what he had expected. The street people didn't know where Lily was but they were working on that. They would alert him as soon as they knew where she was.

Andrew stood at his living room window, lost in thought. He felt the tug at his pant leg and looked down, before bending to gather his young daughter into his arms. She hugged him tightly and began to chatter away, looking over his arm at the calico cat who sat looking up at her. Phoebe, Andrew's wife, approached, an arm around her husband.

"Any word, Drew?" Her voice held her concern. Lily had become a good friend to her.

"Not a word. We don't know where they are or who or why. Bill and Jason are working on different aspects of it. We just don't have what we need right now to find Lily and the others." Andrew didn't continue. He didn't need to. Phoebe knew how he thought and felt. All they could do was pray. And that they were doing on a constant basis.

Two days later, Bill was on the move. He had word as to where Lily was being held. The people on the street had come through. He sent Jason to obtain the warrants that were needed as he himself headed to find Andrew.

"Andrew? We have word where Lily might be. I'm setting up a team to go in." Bill stood in Andrew's doorway, watching as Andrew's head raised. "I'll keep you in the loop."

"Do that. I'll find her family once you've confirmed that you have her and the others." Andrew hesitated for a moment. "What about Longfort's family?"

"He's an orphan. His family died in a car accident when he was about four. His aunt raised him but she passed away a year or so ago from cancer. He has no family that we can find." Bill disappeared, heading for where the team was waiting. The team left their headquarters, heading for an industrial site on the other side of town.

Bill parked his car down the street from the building, his eyes on it. He waited somewhat impatiently for Jason to appear. His head turned as his car door opened and Jason slipped inside.

"I have the warrants, Bill. The judge was very glad to sign them. He just cautioned us to not make too many waves against the building owner for now." Jason had the warrants tightly clasped in his hand.

"Okay. Let's pray before we head out. God has to be the One who leads us. Too much can go wrong if we don't follow His leading."

"That's too true, Bill. We've seen it too many times over the years."

Out of the vehicle at last, Bill gathered the team around them. The emergency task force wa present and would take the lead in going in. Some of the officers present would surround the building. Others would follow the team as they headed in. Bill studied each officer, seeing the determination on all of the faces to find Lily and bring her back to their group. She had been missed greatly by all of them. She had a way of listening and advising when asked that had endeared her to each one.

The ETF team moved in, shouts that it was the police and to come out. There was no response or movement detected. Bill had his eyes on a locked door to one side of the building. He headed that way, following the ETF. The door was broken in quickly and flew open, startling them all for a moment. The team was through the open door, their weapons down in position before being pointed to the ceiling.

Bill shot through the door, Jason on his heels, before they slid to a stop. Lily stood in front of them, shock and then happiness flittering across her face. She looked a little worse for the wear. She turned from them and dropped to her knees beside the stretcher.

Watching Lily for a moment before his eyes raised, Bill took in the area around them. A frown planted itself on his face as he saw what seemed to be an operating room in the corner. His gaze then turned to the paramedic who stood watching them and then to the two physicians. They were alive, he thought, thanking God for that. He walked forward to lay a hand on Lily's shoulder. He felt the shudder that ran through her before she spoke.

"We need to get Loch out of here, Bill. Doc here did surgery on him but he needs further care." Lily was on her feet, watching as the men raised the stretcher and then shifted it to the rig. Jason slid behind the wheel and watched through the window to the back as the paramedic and the surgeon slid inside. The other paramedic slid behind the wheel, taking off at full speed.

Chapter 5

Lily sat on the edge of a stretcher in the emergency room. She didn't want to be there. She wanted to be where Loch was. She was very worried about her friend. Lily didn't want to lose him now that he was back in her life. Her eyes raised as Andrew appeared in front of her and she frowned at him.

"Lily? You're okay? You weren't mistreated?" Andrew's voice was soft, showing the concern that he felt, something that he felt for all of his officers and civilian employees.

"No, I wasn't. They locked us in there and then we were joined by the physicians. Loch needed surgery to remove the knife. He's in bad shape, Andrew."

Andrew nodded. He had already tracked down the emergency physician and spoken with him.

"I know. Tell me. How do you know him?" Andrew waited patiently for Lily to gather her thoughts.

"Loch? We were friends throughout school. His aunt was our neighbour and took him in when his parents were killed. He's had a tough life, Andrew, but his faith was one of the strongest ones that I have seen. Loch prayed about absolutely everything. He told me once that he had a lifelong, daylong conversation with his Abba Father. He's right. That's what I'm trying to do. I walked away from my parents' faith years ago without believing. Now that I do, I want to be like Loch."

"I see." Andrew had observed the change in Lily over the last few years and knew that her words were true.

"How is he, Andrew? I need to see him." Lily made a motion to slide from the stretcher, stopping as Andrew's hand went up. "Andrew?"

"You can't at the moment, Lily. The physicians are with him. We'll get you to see him soon. In the meanwhile, have you given your statement?"

"I have. Not that there was much to give." Lily looked troubled. "Who and why?"

"We don't know yet, Lily. You understand only too well how this works." Andrew turned as he heard a sound outside of the doorway. "Your brother is here."

"Luke? I was praying that he stayed away." She looked gloomily at her brother as he entered, still in his firefighter uniform. "Luke?"

Luke Gordon studied his sister from where he stood in the doorway before he was across the room and hugging her tightly. He and his friends and team mates had searched for her without finding her. He was grateful that God had brought her home, relatively unscathed. He leaned back to look down at her, a frown on his face.

"Lily? Are you okay?" His voice was low. The siblings were close but at this point in their lives, they were heading in different directions.

"I'm not sure any more, Luke. Have you heard how Loch is?" She looked up at her brother.

"Loch? Loch Longfort? How does he fit in?"

"He was there. He was stabbed, Luke. I'm not sure if he'll make it." Lily blinked back tears before leaning back into her brother's hug. "I was on the crime scene at his building when this all happened. I don't know who stabbed him or who took us captive. I want them."

"So do I. We'll pray it through, Lily. We'll pray it through. Our people are looking out for you and searching for whoever it is. They won't stop even though you're home." Luke stepped back from his sister, waiting for her to slide from the stretcher and walk towards the door. He followed her, knowing that she was looking for her friend from years ago. Luke knew that Lily had always had a soft spot in her heart for Loch over the years and that she had been saddened greatly when he had left town and not returned. He frowned, wondering how Loch had appeared without them knowing about it.

Lily searched for Loch, standing in the hallway staring into the room before her feet carried her forward to stand at his bedside. She didn't like the gray look on his face or the blueness around his lips. The surgeon had tried his best but he didn't have the equipment or medications that he needed to treat Loch. She prayed for her friend, devastated that he might not make it after all. Lily felt an arm around her and turned to find the physician beside her. He too was a childhood friend of both hers and Loch's.

“Jamie? How is he?” Lily’s voice was barely audible.

“Not great, Lily. Not great. They’re getting ready to take him back into surgery. Joseph did the best that he could under the circumstances. We all understand that. It’s just that Loch needed more care than he could provide.” Jamie paused. “I don’t understand any of this, Lily.”

“None of us do. This was no way that I could see who attacked him. And I don’t know why the rig was taken. It’s not making sense. What or who were they after?” Lily’s hand reached to rest against Loch’s cheek. She was dismayed at the heat that she felt under her hand. “He’s got a bad fever, Jamie.”

“He does, Lily. He’s fighting a severe infection.” Jamie’s head turned as he heard footsteps. “They’re here to take him to the operating room. You can see him afterwards. Right now? You need to head home and get cleaned up. Go on with Luke. I’ll make sure that they call you when it’s done.” Jamie watched with compassion the struggle that Lily was undergoing before she nodded and walked away, Luke waiting to wrap his sister into another hug.

Bill had been watching before he approached Jamie. Jamie turned as he sensed someone beside him.

“Bill?” Jamie didn’t say anything more.

“How is he?” Bill had a suspicion about how Loch was. He didn’t want to voice it.

“Not good. They’re not sure if he will make it through surgery. If he does, he has a long road to recovery ahead of him." Jamie walked away, leaving Bill looking angry before he too walked away, heading for his car and his office.

Lily was back at the hospital within an hour, Luke beside her. She sat and watched the door to the operating rooms, not willing to let Loch be there on his own. She owed him that much, she decided, before her thoughts turned to prayer and she begged God to heal her friend.

Chapter 6

The surgeon turned at last from monitoring Loch's condition. He had been sure numerous times that they would lose Loch. He could feel the prayers of the community as he worked away to save a man's life. Heading for the waiting room, Paul pulled the surgical cap from his head. He was exhausted with the surgery tedious and time-consuming. He was aware that Loch didn't have any family left in town. The operating room ward clerk had advised him that Lily was waiting to speak with him. He had nodded, knowing that Lily and Loch were old friends and neighbours.

Paul hesitated as he stepped through the doors to the operating suite and headed to where he could see Lily on her feet. Luke was beside her and he could see Bill flanking her as well.

"Paul?" Lily's voice held the hope as well as the fear that dominated her emotions.

"Lily? Let's have a seat. Yes, I'll talk with you. Bill needs to hear this as well." Paul sat, a deep sigh rising within him. "Loch is in recovery right now, Lily. He'll be heading for the Intensive Care Unit once he's able to be moved. And we'll get you in to see him. I remember that you and he were good friends."

"We were, Paul." Paul was a friend from church who had always taken an interest in the teens over the years. Lily had always appreciated his wisdom. "How bad?"

“Bad enough. We cleaned up the wound and started him on the medications that he needs.” Paul didn’t go into the details of how they cleaned the wound. Lily didn’t need to know that. “If you have any questions, I’ll be around for a while.”

Lily nodded as she watched him walk away. She knew that Luke and Bill were sitting on either side of her. Bill had taken her statement, disturbed at what she had said.

Her mind drifting back to that morning, Lily frowned as she studied the gray tiled floor. She had not expected anything such as what had happened. Her concern had been on Loch as they had set off from the crime scene and headed for the hospital, a trip that never did get completed that day. Her head had been aching as she watched the paramedic, Daniel, work on Loch. Lily could tell how worried he was by his actions.

The paramedic rig had come to a sudden stop, surprising both of them. Lily could hear subdued conversation from outside of the vehicle but couldn’t see the men. The fog had not lifted enough for that to happen. She had shared a look with Daniel who had shrugged, his attention going back to Loch. Daniel was worried about him. He didn’t disturb the knife, knowing that it couldn’t be removed until a surgeon had seen Loch and diagnostic imaging was done to assess the damage.

Lily frowned as she felt the twists and turns of the vehicle. It didn’t make sense. She tried to see the driver but couldn’t quite make out his features. He didn't seem to be the paramedic but she could not be sure about that.

They could feel the rig slowing and then heard the sound of the motor become more muffled as if they had entered a building. Daniel and Lily exchanged puzzled glances. They didn't think that they were at the hospital but could not tell.

The vehicle stopped and then shifted as the driver dropped to the ground. Lily watched the door intently, sensing danger and not knowing why. The back door opened with a jerk, startling Daniel who jumped, his eyes on the men who stood outside looking in at them. His partner was not there. His mouth opened to speak before he snapped it closed.

"Out of there." The weapon pointed at him had him dropping to the concrete floor of the building and reaching for the stretcher. He pulled it out, one of the men stepping up to help him. He grimaced at the pain that crossed Loch's face.

Lily carefully dropped to the floor, finding her weapon removed from its holster. Her face harden as she searched the men's faces. This was not what she had expected nor wanted to see. She was roughly shoved forward towards a door, the stretcher wheels squeaking behind her. Daniel had been made to stay behind. He was ordered to pull what he needed from the rig and then too was shoved towards the room. The door slammed shut and they could hear the sounds of locks being snapped shut.

Lily spun and ran for the door, tugging at the handle even though she knew it was futile. She searched the room, which was sterile looking with little furniture and a two-piece bathroom. She opened the small fridge and found water inside it but no food. Looking up, Lily studied the windows, knowing that there was no way that she could reach them or even get out of them.

Daniel's attention was on Loch. He was assessing him and trying to make decisions on what he could do for him. He was well aware that Loch needed more attention than he could give. It was obvious that was not happening. Daniel began to pray for Loch, begging God to keep Loch alive. Daniel didn't want Loch to die on his watch.

Lowering the stretcher, Daniel continued to work on Loch. Lily was on her knees beside him, her eyes worried.

"What can I do, Daniel? What do you want me to do?" Lily reached for the packages of bandages that Daniel was pulling from his kits.

"You need gloves. Then I need you to help me keep Loch alive." Daniel's attention was on the wound. There was not a lot of bleeding but he was concerned about that. He knew that Loch would very well die on him from internal bleeding. He would do his best to keep that from happening.

"Tell me what to do." Lily was reaching to help. It was not her normal task but she was not afraid to step in as she needed to.

"Pray for him, Lily." Daniel didn't look up but he was certain that was what she was doing. "He needs more help than what I can give him."

"I am, Daniel. He's an old friend and neighbour. I don't know what is going on but he doesn't deserve to be in this condition and not in a hospital.

Hours later, the two turned as they heard the door opening. Shock coloured their faces as they saw the surgeon and anesthetist shoved into the room. Their captor glared at them all before he slammed the door shut once more and then locked it.

Daniel was on his feet, shock still on his face as he faced the surgeon, Peter by name, and the anesthetist, Susan.

"What happened?" Lily was in front of them, questions on her face.

"We were abducted from the hospital parking lot, Lily." Peter knew her from interacting with her at the hospital. "We don't know why."

Lily pointed to the stretcher, Daniel shifting out of the way. She heard the exclamation from Peter and Susan before they were at the stretcher and on their knees. They took with a brief word of thanks the gloves that they were offered.

"How long?" Peter knew that there was a timeline for repairing the damage done to Loch.

Lily told him, standing as close as she could to them. She turned her head as she heard the door open once more and saw the boxes that were dropped inside the door. Waiting for the door to close again, Lily walked over to look down into them. She frowned as she saw the equipment that was in them.

Susan moved to stand beside her, a frown on her own face.

"Equipment for an operation? They don't mean him to die?" Susan's voice held her confusion.

"It seems as if you were taken to do surgery, Susan. And that means that they want to keep Loch alive. I want to know why. This is not making any sense." Lily paced the room, staying away from the stretcher as much as she wanted to be there. Her prayers were lifted in almost a desperate manner. She didn't want Loch to die. She wanted him to live so that she could renew her friendship with him. He had been missed greatly when he left town.

Daniel's gloved hands were in the middle of the operation, acting as the assistant even though he had never done that before. Susan monitored Loch, knowing that he needed anesthesia but they had none to give him. Peter looked up for a moment, thinking that he was back in another country, doing surgery in primitive conditions. That was not how it was supposed to work in Canada. He needed to be in a proper operating room and wasn't.

Lily kept her pacing away from them. She couldn't understand the why's of what had happened. She wanted answers but didn't have them and would not likely have them for a while. That did not suit her. She could only pray that Bill had been alerted to them being missing and that he was looking for them.

Daniel rose at last, helping to clean up the area. Loch was still alive but barely. He had held out a bag for the knife to be dropped into. He walked towards

Lily, who nodded and then reached to write the date on the bag as well as what she could remember of the building. They shared a look before Daniel walked away.

Lily moved to stand beside the stretcher, staying out of Peter's way, her eyes on Loch. She prayed for that man, knowing that was all he could do.

Chapter 7

Hours passed as the group that were locked into that room waited for who knew what. Peter and Susan took turns grabbing brief naps, each one monitoring Loch as the other slept. Their exchanged glances were grim. Daniel helped as he could and as they would let him.

Lily had planted herself beside Loch, not willing to move even when they asked her to. Numerous times either Peter or Daniel drew her to her feet and then away so that the physicians could monitor Loch as best they could. Not one of them understood why they had been abducted. Lily had pulled out her phone at one point, frowning that it had not been removed from her pocket. It didn't matter. She had no cell service to call for anyone.

None of them were sure how much time actually passed as they were held captive. Worry about Loch was uppermost in their minds. His condition was deteriorating despite all their efforts. Peter and Susan had talked. Peter didn't expect Loch to last much longer unless they could get him to a hospital and the proper equipment and medications that were available there.

Rattling at the door had all of them spinning to face it. Lily planted herself in front of the others, determined to protect them as best she could. Her hands were up in fists as the door flew open and heavily equipped men charged into the room. Their weapons were held up into the air as they saw Lily protecting the others.

Lily frowned before she was running towards the officer.

"Chad? You're here? How?"

"We finally found you, Lily. Let's get you all out of here and then Bill and the team will move in." Chad's hand was on Lily's arm to move her rapidly from the room.

The officers moved in on the others, working to move the stretcher out of the room and then to the paramedic rig that was waiting. Peter and Daniel were into the back of the rig and leaving before much could be said.

"We need to head out, Lily." Chad approached her, his helmet tucked under his arm. His hand reached out to steady Lily as she swayed. He took a good guess that she had not been sleeping a lot over the last few days, choosing to stay away and stay on guard.

Lily nodded slowly. Her mind was cloudy, she decided, as she slumped towards the ground. Chad's helmet hit the ground as he caught her into his arms and then ran for the second paramedic rig that was waiting, Susan running beside him. One of the team members reached for Chad's helmet as he shared a look with the others.

Lily's thoughts came back to the present as she rose and followed the surgeon towards the ICU. She was afraid for her friend. Hesitating for a moment to offer up a prayer for healing, Lily walked to stand beside Loch's bed. This was not the first time that she had been in this position and she knew full well that it would not be the last. It was different this time, Lily decided. This was a close friend from her childhood. She had never admitted to anyone that she had had a secret crush on the tall handsome youth who lived next door. She would take that to her grave unless Loch said something first. But it had been his image that she had searched for over the years, refusing to date just because the man asking her was not Loch.

She studied the equipment that surrounded him, life-saving equipment, she knew full well. She was afraid for him, afraid that he would not away and that she would never know why. Lily acknowledged that God was in control. She just wanted to help Him out as best she could in her limited human manner.

Lily's hand rested on the one of Loch’s hands that lay on his chest. She noted that his colouring was no longer gray and his lips no longer had that bluish tinge. Her prayers for healing and understanding continued to rise. She felt an arm come around her for a moment.

Bill had stood in the hallway, intent on Lily and her reaction to Loch. There was something going on there, he decided, more than just police officer and victim. He walked forward to wrap his friend in a one-arm hug.

"Lily? You're okay?" Bill kept his voice low.

Lily shrugged. She had no idea how she was supposed to feel as a woman. She knew how she was to feel as a police officer.

"How's the paramedic?"

"He's improving. We thought that we would lose him. God was gracious, Lily, in saving his life and in bringing all of you out of there." Bill looked around, sensing danger nearby. He couldn't see anyone that remotely looked danger however.

"He was, Bill. That is something that I have to learn over and over. How big God's grace really is." She bit at her lip. "What aren't you telling me?"

Bill sighed. Lily knew him only too well.

"Longfort's building was broken into sometime after you disappeared. His apartment on the second floor is trashed. We have to wait for him to go through it to find out if anything is missing." Bill studied Lily closer. "How well do you know him? I forgot. You're been friends for years."

Lily gave a one-shoulder hug. How could she explain their friendship? Bill would poke and prod until he reached the depths of her feelings if she would let him. Right now, she didn't want him to and wasn't sure if she ever wanted him to.

"We were close friends when we were growing up. I would have said that he was my best friend. We lived next door to one another and spent a lot of time in one another's homes. Luke was a close friend too. He always challenged me to strive for my best. I was saddened when we lost touch during college. That's life, though. It's what happens."

"It does. Now that he's back here in town, your friendship will pick up again, I suspect. Do you know if he had any enemies when he was younger?" Bill was grasping at straws, not sure what to ask or how to ask his questions.

Lily blinked for a moment, thinking back to their youth and high school days. She shook her head finally.

"I don't know that he did. He was always ready to help someone, no matter who they were. He was into sports too, so there could be a rivalry from there that was never resolved. He didn't serve in any student council positions. He wasn't into that."

"I see. If you think of anything or anyone, let me know. You're not investigating the murder any more, Lily. Andrew's removed you. You're too close to it."

"That's about what I expected him to do. He's right. I am too close. It doesn't make it any easier to swallow." Lily glared at Bill as he gave a low laugh. "Now, get out of here. Cora and Michael need you at home."

"They do. I'm heading that way. Cora wants to meet up with you over the next day or so as do Madigan and Phoebe." Bill walked away, not satisfied that he had reached through to Lily.

Chapter 8

Lily almost haunted the hospital corridors over the next few days. Andrew refused to let her work, telling her that she needed time to heal. She had frowned at him as he had grinned at her before she nodded. She walked away and headed for Loch. At least there, Lily found some sort of comfort.

Luke watched his sister carefully as she paced. He had attempted to make her leave only to face her wrath and words as she refused. He frowned. Luke wondered just how deep his sister's feelings were for Loch and he prayed for protection of her heart. He had had a long talk with Loch one day about Lily. Loch had not been real forthcoming about his feelings but Luke had read him. Loch was interested in pursing a deeper friendship with Lily. Only the two went their separate ways, each intent on their own careers that didn't seem to include the other.

Lily walked away from Luke, heading for where she was not sure. She stopped as she saw a pair of shoes in her line of sight and looked up. Silas, their minister, stood in front of her.

"Lily? You really do need to look where you're going." His grin was infectious.

Lily returned his grin. She knew full well that he used humour in situations to relieve stress and sadness.

"I know, Silas. I know." Lily stared at him. "Where's Madigan?"

"In the coffee shop. She's bringing you something to eat. She knows you too well."

"She does and yes, I will accept something to eat." Lily felt Luke beside her. "You're here for something more than to make sure I've had something to eat."

"I am. I'm heading in to visit Loch. Madigan will stay with you and Luke." He walked away, leaving Lily staring after him, her mouth opening and closing.

Luke began to laugh. It was not often that someone stopped Lily in her tracks. Silas had managed to do that. He was grateful for the compassionate and caring minister that they had.

Walking towards Lily and Luke and with her hands full of bags of food and a tray of coffee, Madigan began to laugh at the look on Lily's face. Lily turned with a frown on her own face before she looked sheepish. Luke was not as generous as others would have been and began a deep laugh. The trio found seats and began to eat.

Silas had walked away from the siblings, deeply troubled. He had spoken with Bill and knew just how grave a condition that Loch was still in. He had met Loch for coffee a few times but Loch had not really shared many of his thoughts. That troubled Silas and drove him to pray for his new friend.

Standing near the bed, Silas studied the monitors. He had done that enough to get an impression that Loch was improving. He had a long road ahead of him, Silas knew. His eyes dropped to the other man, finding Loch's hand reaching for the oxygen mask. Silas' hand kept it on Loch's face.

Loch's eyes flickered open and closed as he tried to awaken. He drew in a deep breath, not sure where he was.

"Where am I?" His voice was thick and gravelly from disuse and pain.

"You're in the hospital, Loch. It's Silas with you."

"What happened?"

"You were hurt a few days ago. I don't know all the details." Silas began to pray audibly for Loch, asking for healing and a touch of the Master's hand on his body. Loch's expression of pain lessened as he drifted off into a natural sleep.

Silas' head turned as he heard soft footsteps and a nurse appeared.

"He was awake for a few minutes, Sally. He asked where he was and what happened." Silas was not hesitant about giving that kind of information to the nurses.

"He was? That's a good sign. We didn't expect that for a few more days." Sally made her notes and then stepped from the room, her eyes on Lily. Lily would want to be in there, Sally knew, and they didn't have the heart to say no now that Loch was in a bed on the surgical floor.

Silas walked towards Madigan, sitting beside her and then wrapping an arm around her. He knew that she needed to be here, leaving their young daughter with his grandparents. He watched Lily, knowing that she would be up and with Loch as soon as she could.

"Lily? How do we pray for you?" Silas' soft voice broke into Lily's thoughts.

Lily shook her head, coming back the room. She frowned at Silas for a moment, not quite sure now to answer his question.

"I don't know, Silas. You've been where I am. You've counselled others in cases like this. I don't know how to feel. Does that even make sense?"

Silas gave a grin even as he nodded. He knew what she was saying as did Madigan.

"It does make perfect sense, Lily. Even as a police officer, you do face danger in your personal life. This is your time." He pointed over his shoulder towards where Loch's room was. "You're not isolated from danger. You are well aware of that, more so than some of the rest of us. We will pray for you as we would want to be prayed for."

Lily nodded, accepting what Silas had said. He and Madigan would do just what he said. She was on her feet, excusing herself and walking towards Loch's room. She hesitated for a moment before she walked into the room and came to a stop beside Loch. Her hand reached out to rest against his hair. She was afraid for him, even though she knew that he was improving. She didn't want him to die without knowing why it had happened.

Loch's head turned into Lily's hand, a sigh coming from him. His eyes opened for a moment before he dropped back to sleep, a real sleep this time.

Lily could only pray for Loch. She didn't know why they had been taken or why Loch had been stabbed. That was something that Bill and Jason would be working on. And Lily was determined to investigate as well. She would not sit back and wait for anyone to look into it. Her eyes studied Loch, wondering that her friend was back in life

Chapter 9

Loch was sitting up by the next day despite the pain that he was experiencing. He frowned at Luke, who leaned against the end of his bed. Luke had appeared not that long ago, simply asking Loch to stay with him for a few days. Loch frowned harder at Luke.

"I don't understand, Luke. Why?"

"Because you need to stay with someone for the next few days. And if you don't stay with me, my sister is going to be really mad at us." Luke grinned at him, his gaze moving to where his sister stood in the doorway. He didn't think that Loch knew that she was there.

"Luke? Just what are you up to?" Lily walked towards the bed, a hand reaching for the one Loch was holding out. "Loch? How are you?"

"Hurting. What happened?" Loch had had a conversation with Bill early that morning. He just didn't believe what Bill had to say.

"You stumbled on a body a few days ago. We were talking and you were stabbed. When we were heading for the hospital, we were kidnapped and disappeared for a few days. You were operated on again yesterday. And now, you do need to find somewhere to stay for a few days." Lily let out a sigh. "Your apartment is not in any condition for you to stay there. Besides you won't be allowed to climb stairs."

Loch stared at her. He hadn't understood what Bill had meant about his apartment. He wasn't aware that his apartment was destroyed or that was what he thought.

“Lily? Can we go there?” Loch shoved at the blankets covering him but was too weak to move them.

“Loch, no, we can’t.” Lily was adamant about that. “Give it a couple of days and then we will.” Lily folded her arms across her chest, adamant that Loch was not heading for his place. “You have two choices. One. You stay with Luke. Two. You and Luke stay with me. There’s no option in that, Loch.”

Luke rubbed at his upper lip before he walked from the room, almost walking into Bill. Bill frowned at Luke, seeing the grin on the other man’s face.

“Luke?” Bill shifted to where he could see Lily.

“Lily’s laying down the law.” Luke could not control his laughter. Bill began to grin. “She’s given Loch only two options. I’m not sure which one he’ll take. And neither one involves him staying at his apartment.”

“Somehow, that doesn’t surprise me. Lily takes care of the people who she cares about.” Bill studied Lily, seeing from her stance that she was uneasy. His thoughts were that Lily was afraid and was trying hard to hide it. He had come to know her well from their time together on the detective squad.

“Lily will win.” Luke watched as Lily turned and headed his way. “Lily?”

Lily shook her head and walked on by the two men, heading for the stairs and walking out of the hospital. She paused, her face raising to the sun, before she found her car and drove away. She couldn't handle Loch saying no to her request. She sighed as she pulled to a stop in front of a house, noting that a car was in the driveway.

Phoebe McBeth hugged Lily before she turned her to the kitchen. Andrew and Phoebe's young daughter was with Andrew's parents that day and Phoebe was glad for that. Lily needed Phoebe's prayers and needed them then.

"Lily? What happened?" Phoebe poured them each a glass of juice and then sat near her at the table, a hand reaching for Lily's hand.

"I don't know. I tried to talk Loch into either staying with Luke or them both staying with me. Luke is willing to do that. Loch wants to go back to his apartment and he can't. Not yet. He's not up to climbing the stairs. And why is God allowing this?" Lily wiped at the tears that had overflowed her eyes and trickled down her cheek. She was struggling with her faith after what had happened.

"God allows us difficulties. You know that. Andrew has talked with you over the years, I know. It's what he does for his people. We are not immune from danger. We need to trust and that trust is sometimes hard to grasp. You are also in need of healing, Lily. What you went through does cause damage to us. That's where we need our support group. Madigan and I have been meeting to pray for you. Cora is there as well. Let me pray for you, Lily." Phoebe didn't wait for Lily to agree to that. She just bowed her head and prayed.

Lily's emotions had gotten the better of her and her head dropped to her folded arms. She wept silent tears, her shoulders shaking with the strength of her emotions. Phoebe was on her feet, reaching for a cloth to wring out in warm water and was back beside Lily, tucking it into one of Lily's hands

Andrew hesitated as he saw Lily before he glanced at Phoebe. He had sensed that he was needed at home and headed that way, leaving his desk work for later. Phoebe nodded at Lily before Andrew was pulling back a chair to sit beside her. Bill had reached out to him, telling him that Lily needed some counselling and who would he recommend. Andrew had agreed. He had gone through that himself after his and Phoebe's adventure.

"Lily?" Andrew's voice reached through to Lily who raised her head and then wiped at her face.

"Andrew? You shouldn't be here." Lily was dismayed that he was.

"Lily, you need me here. I'm your chief. You need my support. What you went through was not easy. Talk to me. Tell me what you are feeling. And before you ask, Bill has talked to Loch who has agreed to stay with Luke for a few days."

"Thank you, Andrew. I don't know where to start. It just happened so quickly. And I lost my weapon. That's not the way it should be." Lily didn't know that her weapon had just been found in the building. "I have so many emotions running through me."

"You will do. That's where your friends will come in. We'll find someone for you to speak with. That's not an option." Andrew watched with compassion as she nodded, a sober look on her face. "I have read your statements. You know that I don't usually do that, except for circumstances such as this. We'll find out who it was. You just might not like what you have to go through."

"I know, Andrew. I know." Lily rubbed at her eyes, feeling them swollen and sore. "I can protect myself, I think. How do we protect Loch? And why was he targeted like that?"

"We don't know yet, Lily. We are working through that but you understand only too well how long it can take. Do you want to stay with us tonight?" Andrew knew that Phoebe would have no problem with Lily staying with them.

"No, it's okay, Andrew. I need to get moving. Thank you." Lily walked away, leaving Andrew troubled by her actions. She sat for a moment in her car before she pulled away. She didn't see the car following her as she headed for Luke's home. She needed to be with her brother.

Chapter 10

Two days later, Loch rose from where he had been sitting at the kitchen table in Luke's home. He was in pain and felt the pain centred on his chest. Loch rubbed at the area as he walked through to the bedroom that he was using and then packed the few items he had into the plastic bag waiting on the chair. Luke had gone out, admonishing Loch to be careful. Loch had nodded. He needed to go home whether anyone wanted that or not.

The taxi cab dropped Loch at his building. Loch stared at the stairs before he sighed. He knew that it would hurt to walk up them but he had to. He also needed groceries but had no idea how he would manage that. He was on his own, he knew, and that made what he had don't through that much more difficult to accept.

Loch stopped just inside his apartment doorway. Bill had not been wrong when he said his home had been tossed. His hands rested on the top of his head. He sighed. Loch just wanted to collapse in bed but he wouldn't be able to. He turned instead to the kitchen, hoping that he still had coffee that he could brew. He did, he discovered, and thanked God for that. While he waited for the coffee to brew, he turned towards the living room and then walked through his apartment. Whoever it was had not missed one room in the apartment. It would take forever, he decided, to tidy it up.

A tap at the door caught at Loch's ears. He frowned. He didn't have anyone who would be looking for him who knew where he lived. At least, he didn't think that he did. He stared at Lily as she stood there, Madigan and Silas flanking her.

"Loch? Luke thought that you would run as soon as he left." Lily grinned at him for a moment before she frowned. "You're not steady on your feet."

"No, I'm not. But I have to tidy up this place." Loch turned with a grimace of pain and wavered on his feet for a moment. He felt Lily's arm around him to steady him. He looked around, not sure where to start.

"Loch? May I call in friends to help?" Silas had his phone out, ready to call for help.

Loch shrugged. He hadn't reached out to any of his old friends yet. Any help would be appreciated. He knew from Silas' sermons that this was how Silas related to being God's hands and feet on earth.

"That's fine, Silas." Loch sagged against a wall, Lily frowning at him as he did so. "I don't know that I'll be much help. We need to clean as well." He turned as he heard Silas give a laugh. "Silas?"

"It's okay. Madi's parents have that cleaning business." Silas walked away to assess what needed to be done.

Loch turned his gaze to Madigan, who simply grinned and shrugged.

"I talked to them earlier. They'll be here mid-afternoon to clean. I still work for them part-time." Madigan followed Silas.

Lily could hear their quiet conversation. She leaned against the wall beside Loch, lost in thought for a moment.

"Lily?" Loch's voice caught her attention. "Why?"

"Why what?" Lily turned her head to see Loch with a puzzled look on his face.

"This. Silas and Madigan. Their offer to help. I've been away from this town for years. So why help?"

"Because you are part of our church, Loch. You are a friend as well. Silas has mentioned that he would like to get to know you as a friend as has Madigan. You're friends with Luke and me. That brings you into our friends' group whether you realize that or not. I can guarantee that we will have more help that we need to do this. Your apartment will be back in order in no time. Your fridge will be full. And Madigan's parents and brother will come through and clean it all for you." Lily reached to hug her friend before she headed for the kitchen. Opening the fridge, Lily stared at the contents before she turned for a pad of paper and pen, making a grocery list before she reached for a garbage bag and began to toss food. They could not take a chance that anything had been contaminated.

Luke reached to hug his sister as she worked away in the kitchen. He had received her text message and had then carried up bags of food to refill the fridge and freezer.

"How are you, Lily?" Luke was worried about his sister. She still had not talked to him about what happened and he wanted to know why.

Lily shrugged, studying the concern that she saw on his face.

"I don't know, Luke. I really don't know. We need to talk at some point about what happened. For now? We need to get Loch situated once more. Can we do that?"

Luke nodded, knowing that his sister was avoiding the conversation.

"We talk tonight, Lily. There is no option on that." Luke walked away, heading for where their group of friends had started working away.

Lily watched him before she sighed. She had no idea what to expect over the next days and weeks but she would move forward through the days. She would be back at work on the following Monday, Andrew agreeing to that.

Loch watched the friends as they worked away, laughter sparkling through the work. He gave a half-hearted grin. He just knew that once today was over, he would be on his own once more. He didn't want that. Loch had had twelve years of loneliness and wanted to change that.

Silas moved to stand beside Loch, a hand resting on his shoulder. He simply prayed for him.

"Silas? Why have they come out?" Loch was still puzzled by that despite the four couples who had shown up approaching him. He remembered some of them from high school but had not been friends with them.

"They came because of Lily. She's a good friend to them all. She has also been involved in investigating the adventures that they had undergone. "They want to help out others in need. Today, that is you. Now, Madigan's parents and brother have been through. Your place is back to normal, at least up here. Call me tomorrow and I'll help you with your studio." Silas tapped Loch's shoulder and moved to find Madigan.

Loch was still astounded that they had all reached out to him. Each man and lady had talked to speak with him over the hours that they had been there. He was exhausted, locking the door after them all. Lily had simply hugged him as she left, stating that she had left a meal in the crockpot for him when he was ready to eat. He had hugged her back, dropping a kiss on the top of her head without thinking. Loch didn't see the surprised and then happy look that crossed her face.

Chapter 11

The following week, Lily turned from the crime scene that she was on. It was a strange one, she decided, with no clear evidence of what had happened or who had done it. She made her way back to her office, dropping her jacket over the back of her desk chair. Lily sat, staring at the note book in front of her on the desktop. She rubbed at her temple, a headache beginning. She had been troubled by them since the incident weeks before.

Andrew paused at her doorway before he entered and sat in front of her. He waited patiently for Lily to look up, troubled by the distressed look that covered her face.

"Lily? What's troubling you?" Andrew spoke at last.

"I don't know, Andrew." Lily looked up at him. "I worry about Loch. I keep in touch with him but for some reason, he's not responding to any of my calls. We were friends in our teens. I don't know who he is now but he is involved in my life."

"He is. You both have changed over the years. You need to get to know each other again." Andrew didn't tell Lily that Bill was reaching out to Loch, trying to get to know him. "He's a hard read, but we'll get there with him."

"I know that we will. I just worry about him." Lily didn't say much more.

Andrew rose and walked away, stopping for a moment to pray for her. Duty called him and he walked back to his office, lost in his work in short order. He looked up as he heard a tap at his door a couple of hours later and waved Bill in.

"Bill?"

"This stuff with Lily and Loch? It's not making a lot of sense."

"No, it's not. It's frustrating for us all, I know. Tell me what you have." Andrew listened carefully to Bill. "You really don't have much, do you? The fog that night prevented that. And everything was wiped clean in the paramedic rig and the building. What is the word on the murder that Lily was investigating?"

"Not a lot. We have no identification on the man. He's not from Elmton." Bill was frustrated at that. "If we could identify him, perhaps we could figure out why he was dumped there."

"And he was dumped there. There's no mistake about that. It seems as if it might be related to Loch but we can't prove that, can we?" Andrew's mind was moving through all the scenarios that he could think of. "And I know that you've reached out to the surrounding forces."

"It takes time, Andrew." Bill was on his feet. "I need to find Lily. She wasn't in her office when I came by."

"She was. She's hurting in so many ways, Bill. We need to determine what we can do for her." Andrew knew that Phoebe was reaching out to her as were Cora and Madigan. He was sure others of their friends were as well.

Loch stood in his studio. He had managed to set it back to rights with a great deal of pain and discomfort on his part. He had refused any help from anyone, not seeing the look that Silas and Lily shared. He was too independent to take help again.

He turned as he heard the chime from the front door. He didn't know the man who had entered. Loch didn't move from behind his counter, watching the man as he walked around the room before stopping in front on Loch. The man studied him and then smiled.

"Loch Longfort. Lily is a friend of mine." Richard had a security team who had all gone through adventures as they termed them.

"She is? Who isn't she friends with?" Loch studied him. "You were in high school with us."

"I was. I didn't know you other than from seeing you in some classes. I would like to help you. Lily spoke with me, asking that I talk with you. She's too close to the situation. She could counsel you on what you need to watch out for. That's where I come in. Myself and my team."

"I don't understand, Richard. What team?" Loch frowned at Richard.

"I have a security team, Loch. We do training now but we will step in to protect anyone who needs it. Right now, that is you." Richard walked back around the studio, and in and out of the office and other rooms. "You have a good set up here."

"I worked hard to decide how I wanted it." Loch was still frowning at Richard. "What is it you actually want?"

"I want to protect you as best I can." Richard rubbed at his cheek. "Do you have time for a coffee?"

Loch looked down at his counter. He really didn't but he wanted to hear what Richard had to say. He looked up, praying for guidance in what he needed to do.

"I can make the time." Loch moved cautiously. He was still in some pain, the incision itching and pulling as it healed.

Seated in a nearby diner, Richard studied Loch carefully, seeing the strain that he was under. Lily had not been able to give much information to Richard when she had called him the night before. Richard was used to that. It was how security teams worked at times.

"Richard? What exactly did Lily tell you?" Loch waited almost impatiently for Richard to respond.

"She couldn't tell me much other than that you had been stabbed and that both of you had been abducted. She's worried about you. For Lily to be worried for someone means that she acts. And with you, she has reached out to me to ask for help." Richard didn't say anything for a moment, letting Loch think through what he had said. "We need to talk about what we can do to make your life safer. If you will, let us go through your studio and apartment and update your security system if you haven't done that."

"I haven't but I will. Thank you." Loch sat back, his hands wrapped around his mug of coffee. "Talk to me and tell me what you would do if you were me."

Richard nodded. Loch was reacting as he had prayed that he would. Richard was well aware that they could make all the plans in the world to protect Loch and protect Lily but it was God who had ultimate control of everything. Richard was a strong Christian, not afraid to let it be known. He didn't know if Loch was a Christian or how strong his faith was. All he knew was that their faith would be tested and tested severely in the next few weeks.

Chapter 12

Lily headed for Luke's that afternoon. He had called, just asking her to stop by. He was deeply worried about his sister and needed to play the brother role. She let herself into his house, which was in fact their childhood home. Their parents had retired and moved to another city where the temperature was more to their liking. They would return every few months from Victoria, British Columbia, to visit their children.

Setting about preparing a meal for the two of them, Lily worked away in the kitchen. Her thoughts were not on the meal but on Loch. She desperately wanted to call him but couldn't. He would have to be the one to call her.

Lily had moved through her day with her investigations without a lot of thought for her own safety. She had felt watched over the hours but had not seen anyone. That bothered her.

Hearing the doorbell, Lily frowned at the clock. Her preparations were done for the meal but why would Luke be ringing the doorbell? She glanced out before she pulled the door open.

"Loch? What are you doing here?" She reached out to draw him into the house.

"Lily? You're here? I'm looking for Luke." Loch shivered in the heat after coming in from the dampness of the rainy cold day.

"He'll be here soon. We share a lot of meals over a week." Lily stepped forward and hugged Loch, surprising them both. “Come on into the kitchen. You’re familiar enough with it.”

Loch grinned at her words, matching her grin.

“I am. I spent a lot of time here with you two. I miss your parents.”

“They’re heading here next week for a week or so. They do that every few months. They will be glad to see you once more.” Lily handed him a bottle of what that he twisted in his hands.

“I’m glad that you still have your parents. I miss mine.” Loch’s parents had died within three months of each other when he was young, his father surviving his mother by only months.

Lily looked around as she heard Luke enter from the mud room.

“It was too sudden, Loch. And then you left here.” Lily stared at him, her thoughts muddled for a moment. “Why did you come back?”

Loch shrugged. Lily was why he had come back. He didn’t know if she was dating anyone but she had been his ideal lady over the years. He had hesitated about asking her to date during high school, knowing that neither one of them was ready for that. He had kept track of her since he moved back to town to some extent but building his business had taken time as well.

“I just felt it was time to come home. Dad had owned the building where I have my studio. It had been rented up until about a year ago. It is perfect for my studio and having an apartment upstairs works well. I missed the area and the people, Lily." Loch looked at Luke, finding understanding in Luke's eyes.

Luke nodded at Loch. Loch was interested in his sister. Luke had thought that when they were teenagers. He had caught Loch watching Lily at times and had frowned at that. He shrugged at the thought that now that Loch was back in town, perhaps he and Lily would become a couple.

Their meal completed, Luke bowed his head and began to pray, bringing in all the promises that he could think of that mentioned peace, protection, being hidden by God, and being prayed for. Loch followed him in prayer as did Lily.

Loch looked around when they finished. He felt the peace that God gives to some extent. His mouth opened and closed as Luke rose and then returned with pads of paper and pens.

"Luke?"

"We start working this, Loch. Lily can't officially investigate it but she can work on it on her own and with us. Lily? I spoke with Richard. He and his team are willing to come in and work with us."

Lily nodded, having spoken with Silver and Naomi, the two ladies on Richard's team.

"I talked with Silver and Naomi earlier today. Richard's team is available on Saturday to meet with us. The thing is that there is just no information as to who or why. Loch? Did you or your parents have enemies in the past that you know of?"

"Not that I know of. I have paperwork from Dad and Mom that I am going through slowly. It's not really informative." Loch rubbed at his chest. There was discomfort there and a pins and needles sensation but the pain was gone. "I'll work away on it before Saturday and see if there is anything there."

"That would work. Set aside anything that needs further investigation." Lily's mind was racing, trying to think through what she knew.

Driving home at last, Lily watched the headlights in her rearview mirror. She didn't know if it was friend or foe behind her. She was afraid, she finally had to admit to herself. She pulled into her garage, lowering the door behind her car, and then slipped into the house to run towards the front window. Lily studied her street, not seeing the car and praying that it had disappeared for good.

Drawing in a deep breath, Lily sank to the floor, her head dropping to her upraised knees. Her arms wrapped around her head as she began to weep. She could not help herself. She knew that she was praying and begging God for this to end. She just didn't know what she was praying.

On her feet later, Lily walked back to where she had dropped her purse. She pulled out her phone, scrolling through her text messages. She frowned at the one from Bill, knowing that they would speak on the next day. She sent him back a quick text to confirm that they would meet.

Lily turned away from her phone, leaving it plugged in to charge on the kitchen counter. She yawned. She was not sleeping well, despite her pleas to God for rest. Lily knew why. She was scared, no, terrified, she decided, not knowing if someone was out there meaning her harm. And there was no doubt that someone did.

Chapter 13

The next morning, Lily walked towards where Bill stood waiting for her just outside of his office. He studied his friend and fellow detective and nodded. She was on edge, he could tell, and there wasn't much that they could do to help her, other than solving the mystery surrounding Loch. Bill had talked to Loch many times and neither man could understand what had happened.

"Lily?" Bill's voice was quiet as he spoke, before he stepped to one side and let her enter his office.

"Bill? Have you solved this yet?" Lily gave a quick grin.

"I wish, Lily. I wish that I had solved this. It's only going to get messier as we move forward. I've spoken with Loch over the last few days. He has no idea who would have attacked him."

"What about the body, Bill? I was in on that investigation until I was abducted. Do we know who he was?"

"No, we don't. He had no identification on him and his fingerprints have not come back to a match at all. That's frustrating." Bill handed over a photo. "This is what they took for photo identification."

Lily took the photo, her eyes on Bill for a moment. She looked down at it and frowned.

“He was around town for a couple of weeks. I remember seeing him in the diner. I didn’t know that we would be connected like we were. I thought he was just a tourist or a newcomer to town.” Lily shuddered for a moment. “Was he following us?”

“He may have been.” Bill sat back, his pen tapping on the desktop. He stared around his office, taking in the soft green walls and the certificates and photos that Cora had placed there. He focused on the family portrait that held a place of honour on the bookcase. Bill gave a soft smile at his family before he turned back to Lily.

Lily was watching Bill intently. She was puzzled by what was happening and didn’t know how to ask what she needed to. She was not part of the investigation and needed to be careful in what she asked.

“Bill? What do we do next?”

“That’s a good question, Lily. Unfortunately, we don’t have enough information to continue to investigate. We need to set it to one side.” Bill didn’t want to do that but he would have no choice unless something popped up that would move the investigation along.

“I get that, Bill. It’s not the first time that we have done this. It doesn’t make it any easier.” Lily drew in a deep breath. “As you know, Loch and I were friends during our teens. His aunt and he lived beside us. Mom and Dad were friends with his parents and then his aunt. I don’t like seeing this happen to a friend.”

"I know that you don't. On the other side of the coin as we say, Richard says that his team is meeting with you on Saturday." Bill had not been surprised that Richard had reached out as he did.

"We are. We'll look into what we can and then pass it on to you, Bill. I won't do anything that would halt or harm the investigation." Lily was on her feet, walking away to find her own office.

Bill was on his feet as well, moving to the doorway to watch her walk away. He was deeply worried about his friend and also about Luke and Loch. A frown crossed his face as he turned back to his desk. A hand reached out to call a friend.

"Samuel? How are you?" Bill grinned into the phone.

"Bill? I'm doing fine. What property do you need a title search on?" Samuel was a title searcher and was used to Bill reaching out to him.

"Loch Longfort's. This is the address. I want to know who owned it before he did."

"Already done. I began to work on it when Lily disappeared. I've sent you an email this morning." Samuel hesitated. "How is Lily?"

"Lily? She's hurting, Samuel. She wants to find out who did this. She and Loch are old friends, I gather."

"They are. I can remember seeing them around school and church. I think that there was interest in each other but they felt they were too young." Samuel sat back. "We need to do one of our potlucks, Bill. We haven't done one in a while."

"We do. Have Aideen set it up and include Loch. He needs to reach out to our group. He and Lily are not going to be apart from one another, not if I'm reading it right."

Samuel began to laugh. He and Aideen had discussed Lily and Loch and had the same impression.

"Richard said that his team is meeting with them on Saturday. How be we plan something for then? We can all work on it." Samuel turned from his desk and went to find Aideen. Aideen worked as his secretary.

"Samuel? What are you planning now?" Aideen grinned at her husband as he reached to kiss her.

"We need to reach out to Lily and Loch and then Richard. We can work with them on Saturday. Richard is planning on that. And then we want to plan a potluck. Bill suggested it."

"I see. Then I'll reach out to Jonah and Candace. It will be a big group and they are always ready to host on their farm."

"They are."

Aideen reached for the phone, intent on doing that.

Lily turned from her front door late that night. It had been a long day and she was exhausted. Her briefcase was dropped on her home office desk. She was too tired to even eat and headed for her bed. Her eyes closed as she was in the middle of a prayer. Her sleep was deep enough that she didn't hear the sounds of someone walking around her house and trying to find entry into it. Her security system picked up the movement.

Loch turned from staring down at the empty downtown street. He was worried, he had to admit. He had felt followed that day as he had been out and about taking the photographs that he was under contract to procure. He had repeatedly glanced around the areas but had not seen anyone. His eyes raised to the ceiling as he prayed for protection for himself and for Lily. Loch gave a soft smile as he thought about Lily. He was glad to have her back in his life. He had missed her.

Chapter 14

Loch hit his knees early the next morning, his arms wrapping around his abdomen. He had stepped out of the back door of his studio, shielding his eyes from the bright morning sun. Loch had not seen the men waiting for him before fists had landed into his abdomen. A hand grasped his hair and pulled his head back. His eyes were squeezed tight against the pain.

A sudden shove sent him fully to the ground where he lay in a position that had him sprawled facedown. He didn't hear the footsteps running away from him. He had no idea how long he lay there before he twisted to a sitting position, rubbing at his face. Loch stared around through blurry eyes before he dragged himself to his feet, a hand resting against the rough brick of the building.

Loch pulled the door open and stumbled inside before he stopped to draw in as deep a breath as he could. He reached for his phone, his fingers fumbling as he called for help. His phone dropped back to the counter top as he found the stool he kept behind it and slumped on to it.

Bill looked around as Jason stopped in his doorway, a frown on his face.

"Jason?"

"I just grabbed a call from Loch. He was attacked outside of his building just a while ago." Jason watched as Bill surged to his feet. "Coming with me?"

"I am. We'll see what he has to say but I suspect that there won't be much that he'll be able to tell us."

"I suspect that you're right."

Jason waited for the paramedics to finish their assessment of Loch. He listened to their questions and Loch's pain-filled answers. He walked around the photo studio. Jason nodded, seeing how talented Loch was.

Bill approached Jason, a frown on his face. There had been no evidence outside, other than the bag of garbage that Loch had had in his hands when he was attacked. That was frustrating, to say the least. He looked up for a moment, begging God to provide the answers that would solve this. However, Bill was aware that God was in control and whatever happened? That happened in God's timing.

Loch looked at the two detectives through blurry eyes. He hurt but was refusing to be taken to the hospital. He shrugged off the hands and rose, facing Jason and Bill.

"I didn't see anyone, Bill, Jason. I stepped outside and the sun had blinded me. I was attacked right away. So, what do you want me to say? I have no enemies that I know of. I am a photographer who loves his work and cares for his customers. I have gone back over every contact through my work that I have had. There is nothing there." Loch walked away, heading for the kitchen.

The two detectives could hear water running in the kitchenette, the opening and closing of a cupboard door, and then the aroma of brewing coffee. Bill walked that way, Jason heading out to another crime scene. He stood with a shoulder leaning against the doorframe, his eyes on the floor. He could wait for as long as it took for Loch to speak.

Loch paced the kitchenette in an angry manner. He had no answers for the questions that he knew Bill wanted to ask him. It was Thursday and he could not wait for another day to pass and he could lock up the studio for two days. He sighed as he turned to face Bill.

"I don't know anything, Bill. Honestly. If I did, I would tell you. I don't like seeing Lily in danger because of me." Loch struggled with his emotions.

"None of us do, Loch. None of us ever did when we went through what we did. We didn't want the ones who were important to us to be endangered or face death. You know Jason's sister, Julia?"

Loch nodded. He had been acquainted with her during their school days.

"I remember her. Why do you bring her up?"

"She faced something far worse than death when she and Mark had their trouble. She was kidnapped and beaten every day to break her spirit. It almost worked. It was done so that when she was sent overseas, she would not fight the man who had planned it. It has affected her to this day. She doesn't trust as easily as she should."

Loch stared at Bill in horror. He had never heard Julia's story, losing contact with her when he moved away. He swallowed hard.

"She went through that?"

"She did. Mark is the one who reached through her darkness and brought her back to her family. The same for all that group of eight friends and their spouses. I understand that we're having a potluck on Saturday with them all as well as Richard's team."

"We are. I feel overwhelmed at the number of people who will be there." Loch poured them both mugs of coffee. "How did they do it? Lily has given me a brief outline of what you all faced."

"It was hard, Loch. I lost my first wife when we had been just married six months. My wife, Cora? We were friends during school. She lost her husband on their wedding day. Long story short? We married. We both almost died from our final abduction. We are in love, Loch, understanding that God protected us and led us through the years to become the people that we were meant to be. God is in control of the paths and byways that we traverse. No one can tell us how to trust God. That is something that is individual to each one of us. We may share adventures and thoughts and ideas but they are unique to each one of us. All I know is that God has protected me over the years in so many ways that I don't understand or even know about."

Loch had been listening closely to Bill, his head nodding at times.

"I understand what you are saying, Bill. God has a plan for our lives and a path for us to walk. We can follow His will for our lives or wander away and follow our own, ending up in danger and sorrow. I've done that over the years." Loch beckoned Bill to follow him back to the studio. He stopped in front of a picture of a single raindrop, a rainbow glimpsed in the midst of it. "See this photo? I wasn't trying for it. I had taken a picture of a flower in the rain and this showed up. I had to enlarge and print it. It reminds me of a tear drop and that God bottles our tears. It reminds me of the rain that God sends to refresh the earth. He sends His love to us to refresh our souls. It also reminds me that He calms the storms within and without us. The rainbow? It reminds me of all the promises of God that He never breaks."

Bill was listening closely. He nodded at Loch's words. Loch had expressed what Bill had struggled to understand for years. He also echoed what Silas had said at many times.

Chapter 15

Saturday found Loch reaching for Lily's hand as he walked towards Jonah's home. He was surprised at the number of cars that were parked around the property, not fully comprehending just how many people would be there.

Lily looked down at their hands and then just shrugged. If it felt Loch feel more comfortable, she didn't mind. She waved as she walked up to the front porch, finding Candace waiting for her. Candace reached to hug Lily and then surprised Loch by hugging him too. She took the container of squares that Loch was carrying for Lily.

"Everyone's in the office, Lily. Thankfully it's a large room." Candace nodded that way. "Go on. Richard and Raleigh are on their way. They're the last to come."

Lily walked that way, her hand still tight in Loch's. It had been a warm enough day that they had not needed jackets. Lily paused outside of the office as she heard the laughter and chatter that wafted out of the door. She felt Loch tug at her hand.

"Lily? Who all is here?" Loch was feeling overwhelmed, the stress of what he had been going through almost more than he could handle. He was a person who thought clearly and wanted the answers to whatever it was he was involved in or looking at becoming involved in. That was not happening right now.

"Our group of friends. You know the ones we went to school with. They are all married now. And Richard and his team and their spouses are here. Richard was in school with us."

"He was." Loch felt somewhat relieved but he still had a bad feeling that something drastic was about to happen. That had happened once with him. He didn't want it again but didn't think that he had any choice in the matter.

Richard stood behind Lily and Loch, his eyes thoughtful before he nodded. They were a couple. He had thought that they were a couple in high school. Only that never happened. Now it seemed to be. He felt Raleigh's arm around him as she approached.

"Richard?" Raleigh kept her voice low, a slight smile on her face.

Richard grinned down at her, knowing somewhat how she was thinking.

"He's afraid to face us." Richard's smile widened. "He doesn't remember some of us and others of us he has never met. Come on, sweetheart. Let's break the ice as they say."

Lily turned as she felt an arm around her and stared at Loch as he too turned. She frowned at Richard and Raleigh for a moment before she looked back at Loch.

"Loch? You do remember Richard? Of course, you do. He's been around to see you. And this is his wife, Raleigh. Raleigh, this is Loch Longfort, an old friend of ours. We seem to be off on an adventure that we told you ended with each one of you."

Raleigh began to laugh, bringing attention to themselves. The men were on their feet, heading for Lily and to hug her before greeting Loch. Loch drew in a deep breath. Lily was correct, he decided. He was part of this group from high school. Some he had not gotten to know well but others had been friends.

An hour later, Loch raised his head. They had eaten and then spent time in prayer, bringing Lily and Loch to God and petitioning for their protection and for quick resolution of their adventure. He was grateful for all the reminders and promises that had filtered through the prayers.

Lily was on her feet, heading for Jonah's printer and then helping to sort through all the paperwork. There was a lot, she knew, and more would be forthcoming. Samuel approached her, a hand stopping her from moving away.

"Lily? What do you know about Loch's building?" Samuel had reached out to Bill earlier in the week.

"Not a lot. I know that there was a store in there that sold used and antique items. That closed when the store owner retired. That's been what? Five years?" Lily's brow wrinkled as she tried to remember.

"About that. I worry about Loch living there. Richard said that he was going in with his team and sweeping the building and updating the security system.'

Lily felt an arm around her again, this time Loch's. Loch frowned at Samuel.

"Do you suspect something from Mr. Ames' store, Samuel?'

Samuel shrugged, not sure what to say.

"I don't know, Loch. Bill asked me to run a search on the title, just as part of his investigation." Samuel saw Bill watching him from across the room. "I found nothing out of the ordinary. That building's been in your family for many years."

"I have. I always loved it. Right now, it suits me for my studio and also a living space. I sold the house when I moved away." Loch's face saddened at that. "At the time, I couldn't keep it. Now, I wish that I still had it, but that's beside the point." Loch turned to face the room, seeing the activity that seemed to be intensifying. "They're working hard."

"They are, Loch. Lily here has been a good friend to us all. She worked hard on our adventures without any complaints. The least that we can do is return the favour. And you are part of our group, Loch, whether you want to be or not." Samuel's hand went up as Loch's mouth opened to protest. "You're our friend. We take care of our friends. Any adventure that happens? We tag along just because." Samuel grinned before he walked away, heading for Mark who was waving at him.

"He's right, you know. You are part of our group. You left but came back. God led you back here. For how long? Only He knows. But in the meantime, you are involved in something that needs resolution.

And you just had to drag me along with you." Lily sounded so disgruntled that Loch began to laugh.

"Sorry about that, Lily. I didn't know that would happen. But we are on this path together. God has walked before us, hasn't He? He knows what we will face and who and why. All we can do is trust Him."

"And that's the difficult part. I see so much all the time. Sometimes, I wish that I had taken up another line of work." Lily was quiet after she said that.

"You're burning out, Lily. I'll make it a matter of prayer for you." Loch walked away at that, leaving Lily feeling bereft after his arm dropped from around her. She sighed. She was not in the mood for romance but Loch seemed to have other ideas.

Chapter 16

The next afternoon, Loch drew up a stool to his counter in his studio. Even though it was Sunday, he was there. He felt that he had to be. Loch frowned at the photos that he had printed and was studying. His head raised as he looked around. Something seemed off that day and he couldn't put a finger on what it was.

On his feet, Loch wandered through his studio, a finger out now and then to touch a photo. His photos were more nature and animal than human. It was what he liked to do, those and children. There was something about photographing children in their innocence that made him want to provide the parents with as great a photo as he could. His work had been showcased a number of times and he had the awards to prove how good he was.

Pausing at one particular photo, Loch drew in a deep breath. He had captured an old mill, partly crumbled and damaged. The sun had hit it just at the right angle. It was a favourite of Loch's, a reminder to him that God provided all that he needed. The old flour mill? He decided then that he needed to make a trip back to that town and find it once more, to see if any of it was still standing.

Turning as he heard a tap at the door, Loch frowned once more, pacing carefully to the door and peeking out. He sighed. Of course, Bill would be here. Unlocking the door, he silently stood back so that Bill could enter.

Bill studied Loch, seeing the strain that the other man was trying too hard to hide but not doing that great a job on that.

"Loch? I'm here as a friend, not the investigator. You need that." Bill handed over a bag of food. "Lily said that you not likely had eaten."

"And she would be correct. A bad habit I have when I'm troubled. I just lose my appetite." Loch pointed to the counter. "We can eat there or head upstairs."

"This is fine. I really want to take a look at your photos." Bill roamed the studio as Loch ate, not sure why he had appeared that day to spend time with Loch. God had directed him that way.

"Loch? You do children's portraits?" Bill turned, pleasure on his face. "I want to have one done of Michael."

"Michael?" Loch looked up from his meal. "I don't think that I understand."

"Our son. He's almost three. We've had photos taken of him but none are the quality of yours. So, can we book something?" Bill rested his hand on the countertop, knowing that Loch was studying him.

"I never expected you to be a father, Bill. You just didn't seem that interested in any of the girls in our group."

"I was. It was Cora. But we went our separate ways. When I was at college, on the very first day, I met Elizabeth. We married just as we graduated. I would not have looked at any other woman if Elizabeth had lived. Cora and I reconnected, discovered that we truly love one another, and married."

"What about Wesley?" Loch mentioned Bill's brother.

"He's married with two sons. He works on the county police force." Bill drew in a deep breath. "Talk to me, Loch. Tell me what your thoughts are."

Loch shrugged, not knowing how to respond.

"I don't know, Bill. I have no ideas who it might be. Samuel gave me the title search that he did for you. I was going to ask for that as well. I don't see anything there that sent out a red flag. I knew that Dad was comfortable with who had rented that building and I just continued the lease just as my aunt had done.

When I came back here, the building was empty and has suited me well."

"It has. But at some point, you'll want to live somewhere other than where you work. Tell me, Loch. What are your thoughts? I know that we have discussed this briefly but you must have some thoughts since we all met on Saturday. It was noisy but that's how we are. You fit right in with us, you know. They were all glad that you were there." Bill didn't mention the look that he caught on Lily's face. He decided when he saw it that his friend and fellow detective was falling in love. Bill wanted to reassure himself that Loch still had the character of his teens.

"What do I think? I don't know what to think, Bill. It's hard to pin down anyone. I've gone back through Mom and Dad's paperwork and could find nothing there. Dad did own about six buildings and I inherited them. I am in the process of selling three of the buildings to the renters. Those are here in the downtown area. I don't want the burden of being a commercial landlord. The houses are different. They have good, long-term tenants." Loch's finger rubbed at his temple. "As to what's happening? I don't know. I've gone back over all the clients that I have had. I don't see any red flags with any of them from other towns. I am working through the ones from here and who I know that they are related to."

Bill nodded. Loch was doing what he expected him to do.

"Just let me know what you discover. It could mean the difference between life and death for both you and Lily." Bill walked away at last, not satisfied that Loch had been completely honest with him but there was nothing that he could do or say. Loch had his right to his privacy and Bill had to respect it.

Lily raised her head from the report that she was studying. A frown covered her face. There was something in that report that was deeply troubling. She was on her feet, gathering the report and heading to find Andrew. She needed to discuss the ramifications of what she was reading with him.

Andrew looked up as Lily tapped at his door, waving her inside. He sat back in his chair, patiently waiting for Lily to gather her thoughts and speak. He took the report that she was shoving at him, a questioning look on his face.

"Read this, Andrew. Then I need to talk to you about it. There's something there that I need to understand and I'm not."

Andrew nodded before he began to read the report. He frowned at what he was reading before he looked up at Lily. Lily's attention was on the floor but he could see that she was deeply troubled. The only thing that he could do at the present time was pray for her.

"Lily? What are you seeing in this?"

"A huge red flag about someone we both know. How do I prove what I am reading? And how does it affect both Loch and me?"

Chapter 17

Lily was on the run, hearing thundering footsteps behind her. She sneaked a quick glance over her shoulder and picked up her pace. She prayed that she would find somewhere to hide. Seeing an alleyway ahead, Lily dodged down it and found a hiding place behind a large dumpster. She could hear the pounding footsteps as the man ran past her hiding place. She drew in a deep shuddering breath, trying to catch her breath. Her head went down against the blue metal dumpster, a hand covering her mouth to soften the sounds of her gasps for breath.

The man returned, his fist hammering against the dumpsters as he walked by. Lily jumped and barely contained her scream as the dumpster jumped under his thuds. She listened for his footsteps to disappear before she peeked around the edge of the dumpster. Lily turned and ran for the other end of the alleyway, heading for the police department. She waved at the officers who looked up in surprise as she walked quickly by them.

Her head dropped to her hands as she sat behind her desk with elbows planted on the desk top, a shuddering sob shaken from her. She had no idea who the man was. She had gotten a good look at him. Pulling up a program on her computer, she began to search. Her hand froze on the computer mouse as she found him. And she didn't like what she read about him.

On her feet, Lily reached for the printer and gathered the papers together. She headed for Bill, not finding him in his office. She sighed. This is not what she needed. Lily stared down at the photo, jumping as she heard a voice beside her.

"Lily? Are you okay? You look troubled." Jason had stopped beside her, trying to assess what was going on with her.

"No, I'm not okay. This man?" She held up the photo. "He just chased me down the street. I managed to hide and escape. I don't like what he's done in the past."

Jason reached for the photo, finding Lily shaking slightly as he took it. He frowned before he looked at the photo. He froze for a moment before he looked up at Lily, seeing her still shaking. His hand reached for her arm and pulled her to his office and shoved her down into a chair. He reached for a bottle of water and handed it to her.

"Lily? What happened? Why do you have this photo?" Jason sat beside her, concerned for his friend.

Lily looked up at last, fear still showing in her eyes.

"I was followed by someone. I managed to hide from him. This is him. I don't like what I am reading about him."

"No, I don't either. He is quite a nasty character." Jason read back through the information that he was holding. He was suddenly deeply afraid for Lily but knew that there was just no way that they as fellow officers and friends could protect her at all times. He would certainly be speaking with Bill and Andrew.

"Is he the one after us?" Lily was more afraid than she could state. She wanted whaler it was over with but knew that it just wouldn't happen that quickly. She looked around as she heard footsteps stopping at the doorway and Bill appeared. "Bill?"

"Lily? What happened? Someone got word to me that you were running from someone." Bill took the papers that Jason handed him and read through them. He shared a look with Jason before he perched on the corner of Jason's desk. "Lily? Talk to me."

"I didn't see him, Bill, and I was watching. All of a sudden, I heard running footsteps heading my way, looked around and saw him. I took off and then hid behind a dumpster near the tearoom. He looked for me and then left. Why would he be after me? What does that mean in what Loch and I faced?"

"I don't know, Lily. We'll need to investigate that. Jason will look into it. Now, how do we keep you safe?" Bill frowned as Lily moved restlessly on her chair.

Lily was on her feet, walking towards the door. The two men could tell that she was very angry.

"I don't know, Bill, to repeat your words. You can't smother me when I'm working. And there is no way that I want anyone following me around when I'm off duty." She walked away, leaving Bill with a grin on his face.

"She's right, you know, Bill." Jason also gave a grin, knowing that Lily was back to her normal feisty self.

"I know that she is. We'll figure out something to make that happen. When she's on a crime scene, the officers will watch for her. And she'll be with Luke or Loch as much as she can when she's off duty." Bill didn't rise from where he was seated, leaving Jason watching him closely. "Our meeting on Saturday. Did we accomplish anything? I'm thinking that we did but this is just too bizarre that she was followed like this."

"We did. I've been working through the names as I can. So far, I haven't come up with anything but this with Lily today changes how fast that I work them." Jason sighed. "This is not how today was to go."

"No, it wasn't. For now, Jason, concentrate on Lily and Loch. Let me have a list of your cases so that I can decide who to give them to or if we can hold onto them for a few days. We need to solve this. Lily's in more danger than we realize." Bill walked away, heading for Andrew.

Lily trudged towards her home that night. It was early evening but already getting dark. She paused as she sensed someone on her front porch and reached for her weapon. She backed away as the figure approached before she stopped and relaxed.

"Loch! You scared me!" Lily walked into his hug and held on tight to her friend. She felt as if she had come home, realizing that she was falling in love with him. That love would stay hidden unless Loch returned it and told her so.

"I'm sorry. I didn't mean to do that." Loch tightened his hold on his lady. He too was falling in love, only too scared to tell Lily that. "I brought a meal for us. You've had a rough day."

"I have. We need to talk, Loch. Go ahead and set out the meal. I need to change to my grubby clothes. It's been one of those days." Lily walked away from Loch, leaving him standing and staring at her, his emotions open on his face if she had turned around to see him.

Chapter 18

Loch reached to remove the remnants of their meal, the trash disposed of and the leftover food tucked away in the fridge. He refilled their mugs of coffee before he sat beside Lily, his arms surrounding her.

"Lily? We need to pray, don't we? Something scared you today." Loch waited patiently for Lily to nod and look at him.

"We do, Loch. We do. I need to tell you what happened today but I'm so afraid. And that's not me."

"No, it's not, Lily. You have never been someone who scares easily." Loch tightened his hug on his lady and bowed his head, begging God for protection for her and also a peace in the situation.

Lily raised her head when they were finished, biting at her lip. This was a new habit for her, she knew, but she could not help herself. Today had frightened her more than any crime scene or criminal that she had ever faced.

"Lily? What happened?" Loch reached to gently tuck her hair behind her ear so that he could see her face. He didn't like the look that covered it.

"Some man ran after me today. I think that he was trying to kidnap me but I'm not positive on that. I managed to hide behind a dumpster. When I got back to the office, I researched his name. I know who he is. We both know him." Lily turned to him, her emotions open and raw on her face. "It was Timmy Oakes. We know him from school."

"We do. He always seemed to be watching everyone and that wasn't for their good. We could just never prove anything against him." Loch was troubled by the name. He stared across the room, not seeing the soft peach of the walls or the off-white cabinets.

"He was, wasn't he? I thought that it was just him. I guess I was wrong." Lily shifted in Loch's arms, not wanting to move from him.

"I think that we all were, Lily. He had everyone fooled. How do we find him?" Loch was ready to race out of the house and track him down.

"We don't. I can't. Jason is working on it. He'll find him and bring him in. He has a list of crimes that he is accused of and a few warrants that are outstanding. We need to find out who he is working for. And that will be covered very deeply." Lily grew quiet, content to be held. That surprised her. She had always avoided dating. Loch was changing that and she was glad to have him back in her life. God had granted a deeply-buried wish of hers.

"We can't officially, Lily. But I know you and your friends. You'll continue to work on this whether you're allowed to or not. It's who you are. You can't change that."

"No, I can't change who I am. I want this over for you too, Loch. We're tied together in this whether we want to be or not."

Loch looked at Lily, his heart in his eyes for a moment.

"I wouldn't want to be anywhere else but beside you. We'll figure it out. Now, we need to do something fun this weekend." Loch grinned as Lily turned her head and stared at him. "We do. We've been so tied up in this and with me healing that we haven't gone out on a date."

"A date?" Lily's heart stuttered for a moment. Was Loch for real? "A date, Loch?"

"That's right, Lily. A date. I've wanted to ask you out for so many years. We were good friends in high school. I think that I was afraid to ruin that by asking you out."

"I would have said yes. Okay, so what do we do?"

Loch grinned at her before he dropped a kiss on her temple, surprising her.

"I want to take you to another town for the day. Riverville is where I lived for a number of years. I have good friends there. Up for a road trip?" He continued to grin at her.

Lily shrugged. She had been back and forth to Riverville both on police and personal business over the years.

"I've been there many times. I never saw you there."

"I kept myself hidden, I guess. I travelled a lot and didn't have a physical studio." Loch frowned at her. "I know someone who can help us."

"Emma?" Lily grinned at the look on his face. "We know Emma well. She has been a good friend and valuable resource to us over the years."

Loch stared at her, shocked that Lily would know Emma. Then, he shook his head. Of course, she would. Emma reached out to everyone who was a friend of her friends and certainly to those who were in law enforcement.

"I see. Let's see if they're around or not." Loch was torn. He wanted to discuss what was happening with Emma but he just wanted to spend time alone with Lily.

"Let's leave it, Loch. Instead of Riverville, how be we go to Mistletoe? I hear that there's a festival of some sort there this weekend. I've gone over the years at different times. It's always fun."

"Okay, we can do that." Loch bit back a smile. He had friends there as well who had lived through a time of danger. He would certainly see if he could connect with them.

"Saturday? It would be nice to get away and not have to worry about anything for a day." Lily leaned against him. "Thank you, Loch. This is what you would have planned when we were teens. I've missed that."

"Thank you, sweetheart." Loch dropped another kiss on her temple. "Saturday it is. We'll leave early in the morning. For now, I need to run. Come and lock up after me."

Lily walked back through the house, a dreamy look on her face. Her teenage wish had come true. Loch had asked her out on a date. She prayed for their relationship, not sure where it was headed but she knew Loch well enough to know that this was not just a spur of the moment or random question.

Loch watched Lily's house from his car for a moment. He drove off, his mind not on the traffic around him but on what he could plan for Saturday. He didn't see the truck that was following him and waited for Loch to head up the stairs to his apartment.

Jason nodded to himself. Loch was home and safe and so was Lily. He watched around the area for a while, not seeing anything that concerned him. He knew the two were being watched. The force had not been able to arrest anyone as yet.

Chapter 19

Saturday found Loch reaching for Lily's hand to help her from his car and then locking the car behind him. He grinned down at her, seeing the pleased look on her face.

"Ready to have some fun?" Loch laughed as she nodded enthusiastically. "Okay, where do we start?"

Lily shrugged, feeling uncertain and afraid at the same time. She knew that someone was likely following them and that disturbed her. She wanted to be free of that and just didn't know how to do that. She studied the area around her, glad to be away from her town and with Loch. Lily prayed for their safety that day.

Loch looked around and then began to tug Lily with him as he walked along the sidewalk. Her face was glowing, Loch noted, reminiscent of when she was a teenager. He grinned at her as she pulled him to a stop to study the store window.

"This is so interesting, Loch. I love wandering through small towns and in and out of their shops." Lily laughed at him before she sobered, her eyes on the man standing nearby. She frowned. She did not know him but he seemed to be very interested in them. Lily looked away but when she looked back, the man was gone. She frowned and turned to Loch, finding his attention on someone across the street. "Loch?"

"We've been followed, Lily. I think that we will be somewhat safe as long as we stay in the crowd. It's when we're away from them that we'll be in danger." Loch watched as Lily shook her head.

"It doesn't always work that way. Sometimes, the crowd becomes a cover for someone who wants to do something dire. Let's keep on the move, Loch." Lily had sobered somewhat, some of the pleasure of the day disappearing.

Late that afternoon, Loch stood with an arm around Lily as she stared down into a pond in the centre square of the town. He had been happy that day, Lily the same or an even better companion than when in her teens. He had fallen more in love with her love that day, finding her shooting him similar looks. Loch sighed to himself. At some point, he would need to speak with her. He was just afraid that she would run from him and he would lose her to his life.

"Loch? We have to head home?" Lily sounded plaintive as she spoke.

"We do, Lily. We do. We'll come back in a few weeks. Mistletoe has a different festival every month. And I promise to bring you to their Christmas celebration." Loch looked around as he felt someone watching him but could see no one who was obvious. He tucked Lily into his car and then moved to slide behind the wheel.

Loch entered the line of traffic leaving town and then headed towards their home. Night was falling as he did so. His head moving from side to side, he watched carefully for anyone following them. Headlights shone as cars moved towards him and behind him. He drew in a deep breath as he felt danger approaching them. Loch just couldn't see which car it was.

Monday morning found Jason on a search. Lily was not in the department and should have been. They had agreed to meet that morning to go over a mutual case and she had not appeared. He stopped for a moment in a hallway and frowned. Jason headed for the parking lot behind the building and searched it. Lily's car was not there. He ran for his car and headed her way. Her car was in the driveway but she didn't answer any knocks at her door. Jason had a thought and then rapidly drove towards Loch's. He spotted Loch's car but his studio was still locked tight and there was no answer at his apartment door.

Jason was worried more than he thought he could be. He reached for his phone, calling for assistance.

Bill moved quickly through the building, having heard that Lily was missing. He headed for where he knew that Luke would be, waiting patiently until Luke looked around. Luke paled and then walked rapidly towards Bill, his eyes worried.

"Bill?" Luke threw his cup of coffee into a nearby garbage container. He paled even more at the grim look on Bill's face. "Lily?"

"When did you talk to Lily last?" Bill's hand drew him to a nearby bench and shoved him down.

"Lily? Friday night. I was away over the weekend at a conference. She said that she and Loch were headed for Mistletoe on Saturday. She sent me a text about midday asking how the conference was and said that she was having a really great time. She sounded more like she was as a teenager. She's in love, Bill."

"I know that she is. So is Loch. They make a great couple." Bill hesitated. "We can't find them, Luke. Her car's in her driveway but there's no answer at her door. The same with Loch's. We're starting a search but we don't know where they are at present." Bill's hand on Luke's shoulder kept him in his seat. "This is a difficult time for you once more. We will find them, Luke. This is where our faith comes through. We need to trust that God has them in His hands and will protect them."

Luke nodded soberly. He was well aware how his faith was being tested. He was also fully aware that Lily and Loch might come home but it would be funerals that they were planning. He didn't want that. Luke choked back his sobs, overcome for a moment.

"What can I do?" Luke's voice was tear-filled and low. He could barely get out the words before he turned to Bill. A hard, angry look was in his eyes.

Bill nodded. Luke was reacting just as he suspected that he would.

"For now? Keep your phone charged and with you. Don't mute it. They may reach out to you."

Luke nodded, his thoughts racing as to where to search. Mistletoe seemed to be it.

"Are you thinking of heading to Mistletoe?" Luke waited for Bill to think through his question.

"Jason has headed that way now. There was a festival there on Saturday so it's doubtful that anyone would remember seeing them. It just puzzles us that their cars are here." Bill prayed for his friends and then rose, heading back to the department and to find Andrew. They had expected that an attempt to kidnap Lily or Loch or both of them would take place. This had taken them by surprise.

Chapter 20

Bill looked up as Jason spoke from his doorway. He waved him in and watched as he sat. He could tell the frustration that Jason was trying hard to deal with.

"Anything?" Bill spoke, not sure if Jason had found out anything.

"They were in the diner there. The owner saw them. They were also spotted in some of the shops. Nothing after late afternoon though. From what I gather, Loch had driven. We don't know if they made it home and disappeared."

"Or disappeared on the way home and his car was returned to his place." Bill sat back, his face thoughtful. "How do we find that evidence?"

"I have someone searching for any video feeds that we can access. They have some and are on the way in with them. I don't know if they'll help, though." Jason was on his feet, a thought troubling him. What if Loch and Lily had disappeared on their way home? How would they ever prove it?

Jason looked around as a patrol officer approached him and handed him some thumb drives. He saw the look on the officer's face and sighed.

"Not Loch?"

"Not Loch. We can't get a real clear look at whoever it was but it wasn't him." The officer was frustrated as well. "Where do we search now, Jason?"

Jason shrugged. He had no idea where to search. And that worried him more than anything. He had reached out to the county force, knowing that Bill and Andrew likely had as well. Both those officers had been on that force before taking the duties of detective and police chief for Elmton.

Andrew paused as he walked through the department, speaking with each officer and civilian employee. They had been through something similar with both himself and Bill. They didn't need it again, he knew, but he also knew that God had allowed it. It was up to them to find Lily and Loch. He approached Jason as that man stood in the break room, staring at the coffee pot as it perked a fresh pot, a bleak look on his face.

"Jason? What do you know?"

Jason looked around, not surprised to find Andrew beside him.

"I don't know, Andrew. I really don't know where to look or who to talk to. I was in Mistletoe earlier and know that they were there until late afternoon. I think that they disappeared somewhere on the drive home. I just don't know where."

"None of us do. I heard from the captain of the county force. His patrols are on the watch for any sign of them. Lily has gone above and beyond many times with their officers. He is also putting out word in the surrounding communities and in the rural areas for people to be on the watch for the two."

"It's frustrating, Andrew. I know that God has a plan and purpose. I just don't see it. And Luke is hurting. He called a few moments ago, just asking if we had any word. It hurt to tell him no."

Jason was awake early the next morning. It was his day off and he had called in their group of friends. Silas stood in the centre of the group, his head bowing as he prayed for them. Their ladies had gathered at Silas' house, praying for the couple. The men, including Luke, had gathered at the church, ready to head out and search the roads back from Mistletoe.

Luke shifted restlessly his feet, wanting to be out looking but also wanting to stay at Lily's and wait for word to come that she was safe. Luke knew that God understood what he was going through and was present with him in this. He could only pray for his sister and Loch. He had no idea where they were or if they were alive or dead. That troubled him greatly.

Silas raised his head to study their group of friends. He frowned as he did so. Bill's brother, Wesley, had appeared. Silas nodded. That was who Wesley was. If there was a need for him to be there and he could be, then that's what he did.

"Wesley?" Jason moved to stand beside him. "You're here?"

"I am. Bill can't be. We talked last night. Our guys are searching as they patrol. I know that some of the men and ladies here are heading to Mistletoe to search. Bill handed over a pile of flyers for them and for us. I know that there are men and ladies out here in Elmton searching. What do you know?" Wesley's heart was heavy for his friend, Lily. He had met Loch at some point, having him take portraits of his boys.

"I know. We had a brief meeting last night with Andrew. Bill's coordinating it here as he can, depending on where he's at with his investigations. We'll find them, Jason."

"I know. I just pray that they're alive." Jason was worried about the couple. He had seen too many times when someone disappeared and either didn't return or came back only for the family to have to bury them. He didn't want that for Luke or Lily's police family.

"That's what we're afraid of, Jason. None of us want this for you. Now, I'm riding with Silas. You're with Luke?"

"I am. The others are splitting up in twos as well." Jason drew in a deep breath. "None of us understand any of this, Wesley. Not one bit. Not the murder that started it all off or what happened right after that. There are no clues that we can find. And there has to be something somewhere." Jason rubbed at his neck. "Not even the people on the street have information for us, and they would come forward if they did. Lily has treated them all fairly, even when she was on patrol and had to arrest them for something."

"She's like that. She has a compassion for people that we don't see to that depth a lot." Wesley walked away to find Silas standing near his car. "Silas?"

"Wesley? I'm glad that you're here. We need to find those two and quickly. I fear for them." Silas did not break Loch's confidence. They had spoken many times over the past few weeks. He appreciated the fine sense of humour that Loch had but also the compassion and caring that had Loch traveling back to Riverville to help out in the homeless shelter when he could.

Wesley nodded. His fingers tapped at the steering wheel. Where were they? He had no idea but knew that their prayers would be effective, in God's timing. They would find the couple. He just didn't know what shape that they would be in. Having seen too much on his patrols and then working directly with a drug task force, he was afraid and deeply afraid.

Chapter 21

Jason pulled his vehicle to the side of the highway, a frown on his face. There was something off about the area. He was out of his car, Luke with him, as he stood for a moment searching the area. He walked forward, following the grass that was still broken down and flat.

"Jason?" Luke had remained on the shoulder of the road at Jason's request. Jason kept to the side of the broken grass, his eyes intent on what he had found.

"Just a moment, Luke." Jason stopped short before he moved carefully forward. He sighed. That was Lily's jacket. Where was she? He turned and walked back towards his car, shaking his head at Luke.

"Jason?" Luke shifted to watch Jason before he glanced back at the area where Jason had hesitated.

Jason reached for his phone, calling Wesley and then calling the county force. He was disturbed at what he found. It was what he had expected but had not wanted to find.

Wesley walked towards Jason who nodded away from his car. The two officers stopped, watching the activity that was increasing in the area.

"Jason? What did you find?"

"I stopped because something told me to. That had to be God. I followed the broken grass. Lily's jacket is there but she's not. And I don't see any sign of Loch." Jason was troubled, his phone clenched in his hand. "How do I tell Luke?"

"You don't. You call Bill and Andrew. They'll do that. You've given him the basics, I suspect, and he'll have decided that his sister was here. He'll wait for you to speak with him. It's who he is."

"He will. And I'm afraid for them, Wesley. I don't know if we'll find them in time."

"That's always a worry, Jason. And you're doing God's work for Him. Let Him have your worry." Wesley knew just how hard it was. He had gone through all those emotions when Bill and Cora had had their adventure.

"You went through this. You need to speak with Luke. Tell him how you felt." Jason looked past Wesley to see Luke staring at them in shock. "Luke?"

"What are you talking about, Jason?"

Wesley turned before. His hand was out directing Luke to an area that was quieter and where he could speak with him.

"Bill and Cora had an adventure years ago. They both disappeared near the end of it. We almost lost them both due to a drug lord and his minions." Wesley watched with compassion as Luke studied him in shock.

"You did? Okay. I know Jason found something to do with one of them, likely Lily. He's too quiet about what he found. And I get that he has to be. Now, how do we do this? Do we call the others?" Luke was pacing in short steps, agitation evident.

"No, we wait for official word. And we will get that. For now, we just need to stay off to the side and out of their way. Wesley looked at Silas, who nodded before he reached out a hand to draw Luke back towards Wesley's car.

Luke shrugged deeper into his jacket. The air was damp that day, rain threatening from the dark heavy clouds overheard. He watched the activity that had increased, his prayers reaching out to heaven for his sister and her fellow.

Silas leaned against Wesley's car, disturbed by what was going on. He and Lily had talked many times, Lily seeking counselling over the years after what she had encountered during her investigations and her time on patrol.

"Silas?" Luke turned his head to stare at Silas. "How do we pray? I have no words to pray. I just want my sister back."

"We know that you do, Luke. Any of us would. Madigan and I went through some rough stuff. We married very quickly but she is the love of my life and I'm hers. God is here in the centre of it. He will never leave Lily and Loch. We don't like what we have to go through but God never promised that we wouldn't have difficulties in life. He has promised to be with us, to never leave us or forsake us. He hides us under His wings and in the cleft of the rock where He covers us. I cling to the promise that He never changes."

"Those are wonderful promises, Silas. I have appreciated your messages over the years. You have a sense of knowing what people need to hear, whether it hurts or not." Luke turned to watch the activity again. "I cling to the fact that Christ did that in the garden, when He prayed for us. That has gotten me through some rough times."

"He did that, for sure. And the Holy Spirit continues to intercede for us. Christ promised not to leave us comfortless and the Holy Spirit is that Comforter." Silas stared at the fingers that he was rubbing together, not sure if he should continue to speak or not.

"I don't know how people who have no faith get through times like this. I know that I would be a basket case or a worse basket case than I am already. Lily's my little sister. I promised Mom and Dad when she was placed in my arms as a newborn that I would protect her. And I feel as if I have let them down." Luke was almost in tears at this point.

"No one thinks that, Luke. She's an adult and independent. You can't smother her. She won't let you. And now that Loch and she are dating, you do need to step to one side." Silas grinned at him for a moment.

Luke nodded. Silas had expressed his feelings for him. He did need to step aside and had been doing that ever since Lily had joined the police force. He just didn't want to. Luke was afraid for his sister. He didn't know how to handle that fear. All he could do was pray that God would give him the peace that he needed and that He would bring Lily and Loch home quickly.

Silas nodded to himself. He could see that Luke was hurting and hurting deeply with his sister missing. He didn't know how to help other than to stand beside Luke and pray for the situation.

Jason looked around, hearing a vehicle coming to a stop near him. He nodded. Andrew had arrived. He walked towards Andrew, seeing Bill appearing from Andrew's car as well.

"Jason? What do we have?" Andrew stopped beside Jason, his eyes on the activity around them.

"I found Lily's jacket out there. There is no sign of them." Jason sighed. He didn't know what else to say.

"Her jacket? No sign of her or Loch?" Andrew drew in a deep breath. "Okay. We'll work with the officers here." He watched as Bill walked towards his brother. "Wesley's here?"

"He is. He was in on the search. I didn't expect to find anything though, Andrew. Not at all. I just felt I had to stop here and search. I saw the disturbance in the grass and followed it."

Andrew nodded. He knew how careful Jason would have been.

Chapter 22

Jason trudged slowly towards the police department building three days later. There had been no sign of either Lily or Loch and that was concerning and worrying all of them. The officers were out on their own time searching wherever they could. Friends had taken over the search as civilians, posters going up wherever they could put them. There was just no sign of them.

Bill looked around as he heard Jason's footsteps and waited for him to catch up to him. He studied his friend and sighed. They were both not sleeping, worried about Lily and where she was.

"Jason? Any word?" Bill was hoping that there had been.

Jason shook his head. He was reliving when his own sister had disappeared.

"Not a one. And that worries me, Bill. We know only too well how this works out." Jason stared up at the sullen sky, waiting for the downpour to happen. He didn't want it but he knew it was going to happen despite his wishes.

"We do, Jason. Only too well." Bill keyed in his passcode and walked through the building to his office. His coat was shrugged off and dropped onto the back of his chair. Jason slumped into a chair as he watched Bill sit and reach for his computer.

"Where do we start to look?" Jason was at a loss as was everyone else.

"I don't, Jason. Lily said that she and Loch have not been receiving packages or letters or that sort of thing. She was surprised at that." Bill had had a long conversation the week before about that. He had also approached Loch who had shaken his head when he was asked about it. "No word on the street?"

"Nothing. And if they knew anything, then there would be." Jason leaned back, his eyes closing for a moment. "I spoke with Julia earlier. The ladies are meeting for prayer every morning. Cora, Madigan, and Phoebe are part of that."

"Cora mentioned it. Phoebe's mom has stepped in to watch the kids along with Madigan's mom. I don't know if Lily realizes how much she is loved by everyone who she is in contact with. Well, a lot of the people. We've gone back over her cases?"

"We have. Lily worked on that on her own. She didn't see anyone who had threatened her that would go after Loch. She was working back through our high school classes and college classes. The only thing is that she and Loch went their separate ways after high school until now."

"Loch mentioned that he lived in Riverville. I reached out to Frankie Brennan this morning but haven't heard back from him." Frankie was the lead detective on the Riverville force.

"He did? That means that we can call in Emma Finlay." Jason grew hopeful that maybe, just maybe, they could find out some information. Emma had a business called Trackers that found information and people that no one else could find. And when she was asked, she couldn't explain how she did that.

"That we can. In fact, Emma called me last night, just to catch up. She asked about Loch. I don't know how she does that, knowing when to ask about someone."

"She has that knack." Jason rose and walked away, heading for where, he didn't know. He walked out of the building and then away from it, heading for the downtown area. Something was forcing him that way and he had learned to follow his instincts. He found a seat in a favourite diner, waiting patiently for whatever it was.

Luke stood in the area where Lily's jacket had been found. He had come back to there, thinking that was the last place. He was desperate to find his sister, not wanting any harm to come to her. Luke didn't understand why she had been targeted on a personal level. Luke was convinced that was why. He also didn't understand why Loch had been the victim of crime. He didn't have that sense that Loch was involved in crime.

Timothy, one of Richard's security team, and Zeke, another of their friends, walked towards Luke. They stood beside Luke, flanking him.

"Luke?" Zeke spoke at last, his eyes on Luke's face. He could understand to a certain extent what Luke was feeling. He and Paige had been targeted by a group determined to destroy the area with chemicals.

“Zeke? Timothy? When did you get here?” Luke had been lost in thought and prayer. He had not heard the men approaching him.

“Just now. We were on the way to Oak City and saw your truck.” Timothy shared a look with Zeke. “What are you thinking?”

“That my sister is missing and I have no idea where she is. It hurts, guys.” Luke walked around the area, knowing that it had been searched thoroughly. “I don’t understand this.” He pointed at the tramped down area.

“Lily likely tried to run. She didn’t make it to safety.” Timothy studied the path. “I don’t see that Loch was with her. He may have sent her on her own.”

“That’s what I was thinking.” Luke stared up at the sky. “How do we find them?”

“It’s going to be difficult, Luke.” Zeke knew that only too well. “Let’s go find somewhere to grab a meal and we’ll talk and pray.”

The three men slid into a booth in a local roadside diner, nodding at the server as she approached with three mugs and the coffee pot. Their orders were placed quickly before Zeke just bowed his head and began to pray for the situation, Lily and Loch, and then for Luke. Luke could feel peace beginning in his heart, knowing that God was there with his sister and her fellow.

Timothy watched Luke carefully for a moment. He sighed. This was not a spot where Luke needed to be in his life. He shared a look with Zeke before he reached for his mug of coffee.

"Luke, you're not going to want to hear this but we need to ensure that you are safe. If Lily refuses to cooperate with her kidnappers, chances are that they'll go after you to make her do so." Timothy watched as Luke stared back at him.

Luke nodded. He got that. He had already been warned many times about that by Andrew and Bill. He didn't know how to stay safe though.

Chapter 24

Jason ran for his vehicle two days later, Bill running with him. Word had come in to the department that someone had found Lily and Loch. They weren't sure that it was correct but they could take no chance that it wasn't correct.

Shutting the car doors quietly, Jason and Bill crept towards the building. It was an abandoned one just on the edge of town. They shared a look before they ran quickly across the debris-strewn and overgrown parking lot, crouching low in an attempt to stay as unnoticeable as they could.

Bill's hand reached for the rusty steel door, pulling it open enough so that he could squeeze through. Jason followed, his weapon clasped in both hands. They shared a look before they began an active step-by-step search. They found nothing. Holstering their weapons, the two detectives walked back outside to the parking. Bill stood for a moment, staring around. The tip had been credible, they knew. Just where were the two?

Jason stood for a moment before he turned in a circle. He was vaguely familiar with the property and the surrounding properties. His hand went out to stop Bill from walking away.

"Bill? There are properties that are attached to this place. Do we search them?" Jason waited almost impatiently for Bill to study the surrounding area.

"We will need to but we'll need the search warrants for them. And I don't know that we have enough information to get them." Bill walked towards Jason's car and stood with his hand on the open door. "Let's see what we can dig up." He sighed as his phone chimed and he pulled it out. "Scrape that. You can work on that. I have a meeting to get to that I didn't plan on."

Jason turned from his computer later that day. He had worked on searching the properties between his other investigations. He was frustrated. He had not been able to find enough information to warrant going before a judge to obtain the search warrants that they needed.

Bill stood for a moment at the front desk, staring at the officer who was manning the desk. He then reached for the envelope that was being handed to him.

"Who dropped it off?" Bill was frowning at the envelope, seeing his name scrawled in dark ink seemingly written by an unsteady hand.

"I'm not sure. I turned away for a moment to see to someone else. There were a few people who had come in at the time. I thought that I saw Old George leaving."

Bill nodded. Old George would have done it in this way, he knew. He also knew that there would be no way that he would find that man in the next few days unless Old George wanted to be found.

Andrew stood beside Bill as that man studied the envelope.

"Bill?" Andrew's voice roused Bill from his thoughts.

"Andrew?" Bill held up the envelope. "This just came from someone. I suspect it was Old George."

"What is this about?" Andrew followed as Bill headed for his office to pull on latex gloves.

"I have no idea." Bill studied the envelope before he reached for his phone and called for a crime scene tech. "We need to do this properly, no matter how much I want to open it."

The two men stood back and watched as the tech opened the envelope and then the letter, carefully testing for any trace of any evidence. She then handed the letter to Bill, the letter and envelope both sealed in individual evidence bags.

Bill thanked her and watched her walk away before he looked at the letter. He read it through and then read it again before he passed it over to Andrew. Andrew frowned at Bill before he read the letter.

"Bill? What are your thoughts?" Andrew's voice broke the silence at last.

"I don't know, Andrew. I really don't know. It says that the writer knows where Loch and Lily are and will work to get them free. We have no way to prove or disprove this. And we need to do that. We should be the ones moving in to rescue them."

"I know, Bill. It's what we're trained to do. But we don't know where they are." Andrew was frustrated.

“We would. I’ll keep working on this. Jason was working through the properties surrounding that one.” Bill frowned at the letter. “This is not making sense, Andrew.”

“No, it’s not making sense. We should be able to find information on them or at least why they’re going through what they are. We’ve looked into Lily and Loch and their families?”

“We have. We’ve gone back as far as we can and found nothing. Luke has been a source of information from their school days. I spoke with Frankie Brennan. Loch lived in Riverville for years. Frankie was not close friends with him but he knew him from church. He also knew his business and said that there were no issues that he was aware of.” Bill looked around as Jason cleared his through. “Jason?”

“Luke mentioned that name when I spoke with him about an hour ago. I’ve looked into her. She is bad news but I’m not sure how it all relates to this.”

Bill took the paper that Jason was thrusting at him and read the name. He frowned. He knew the lady. She was around their age and had been trouble forever, if Bill remembered correctly.

“Her?” Bill watched Jason nod. “What do we know about her?”

“Not a lot at present. I have one of the patrol officers heading for her home to bring her in just for questioning about another matter.” Jason pointed at the letter that Andrew still held. “What’s that?”

“Someone dropped off this letter.” Andrew handed it to him. “What are your thoughts?”

Jason read through the letter, a frown crossing his face. The letter didn’t make sense. It was just a bunch of garble, he decided, before he frowned again.

“Is this is some kind of code? The sentences don’t sense.”

“No, they don’t.” Bill reached for the letter. “They seem to be just a bunch of words strung together.” He walked to the copier and made copies for the three of them. “Here, we can work on it as we can. I pray that there is something there that will make sense and help us to find them.”

Chapter 25

Two days later, Jason was on his feet, a look of success crossing his face. He almost ran to find Bill, that man looking around from the whiteboard that he was working on.

"Jason?" He walked towards the other man, frowning at him.

"Here, Bill. Read this. I think I found them." Jason thrust the paper towards Bill.

"What are you talking about?" Bill took the paper, having difficulty grasping it from how Jason was shaking it at him.

"There. Samuel did a quick title search for us. He found these other properties. This one? It's near that other property but under a numbered company owned by that person."

Bill frowned at Jason before he read through the paper. He read it again, this time pulling out a chair to sit. He stared across the room, staring at the whiteboards that were covered with writing. There was more than one case on the go in the room, with other detectives and officers moving around. He listened to the chatter between them before he looked back at the paper.

"How did we miss this? I never knew this and we were both raised in this town." Bill raised his eyes to Jason who was perched on the edge of the table.

"I know, Bill. This has been hidden so deeply. Samuel said that he's still digging, that his work as a title searcher was being used by God once more. He can't explain how he stumbled onto the name other that God led him to that."

"That He did." Bill studied the paper once more. "We don't know for sure that they are there. And we can't go in without search warrants."

"We don't have enough as of now to get them. I'm working on that as well. Sam is working with me. He's come in on his day off to help." Sam was a friend of Jason and Lily's, a patrol officer who was looking to move ahead in the force.

"Good. He knows the town better than anyone I know." Bill was on his feet, the paper handed back to Jason. "Run with this, Jason. Keep me updated as to what you're finding." Bill prayed that this was where the couple was and that they could move in soon and find them and bring them home.

Jason walked rapidly away, finding Sam waiting for him.

"Sam?" Jason paused beside him.

"Jason? That property? I want to go out and take a look around. If I remember correctly, it's rundown just like the other one." Sam waited for Jason to think it through and then nod.

"Okay, let's head out. I pray that we find them and find them quickly. I'm more than a little worried about them. It's been too long."

"It seems that way. Let's see what we find." Sam parked near the building, his eyes searching the area. He couldn't see anyone but he knew that someone had been around and likely still was.

Jason stared at the building, trying to think through what they needed to do. His door was open as he shoved at it. On his feet, he walked towards the building across the over-grown parking lot. His feet felt the rough pavement underneath his feet, the cracks and piles of broken pavement causing him to walk in a zigzag pattern. Sam was at his side, his eyes searching the area around them,

Jason headed into the building, squeezing through a partly-open door. He waved at the dust and cobwebs that blocked his vision before he walked forward once more. He searched the building and could hear Sam moving around as well. A sudden yell from Sam had him running that way. Jason slid to a stop, a hand out to brace himself against a door.

"Sam?"

"They were here, Jason. I recognize Lily's watch. But where are they now?" Sam rose from where he had been crouching down near a pile of cardboard.

"They were? Okay. Walk back out, Sam. We need to get the search warrant for this building. We have the evidence now that we need." Jason walked rapidly out of the building towards Sam's car. His phone was out to start the process that was needed.

Bill walked towards Jason, the search warrants in his hand. He silently handed them to the other detective, his eyes intent on the teams moving forward.

"What else do you know?"

Jason shrugged. He didn't know a whole lot more than what he had said. He was frustrated, to say the least.

"Not a lot, Bill. Sam found Lily's watch and then we moved out. He left it there for the team to take." Jason turned in a circle as he felt someone watching them. "Someone's out there, Bill. I wonder if they're friend or foe."

"It would be nice if they're a friend and can lead us to the two." Bill walked towards the building, his eyes on the ground as he did so. He paused for a moment, studying an area. "We need the team to take a look at this." Bill reached for the small numbered plastic sign that he was being handed.

"Bill? What is that?" Jason bent over to look. "A camera?"

"It is. I'm not familiar enough with Loch to know if it's one of his."

"I'm not sure either. We'll need to take a look at what's on it to determine that." Jason rose back to his full height. "Where are they, Bill? Are they close to here?"

Bill shrugged. His feeling was that they weren't and that they had been moved out of town to somewhere they would never find them. That had happened once in the past when he was just coming on the county force. He didn't want to see that happen to friends but knew that was a real possibility.

"Jason? Check with the airport in Oak City. See if any small planes took off over the last twelve hours and where they were heading. Sam? Do that for the bus company. We've been looking in that but this here?" Bill pointed towards the building. "This makes it more critical that we do this and now."

Chapter 26

The following Monday, Jason was on the move. He had confirmation as to where Lily and Loch were and was ready to move out. He ran to find Bill and Andrew. Both those men stared at him before Bill too was on the move. He ran for the Emergency Task Force leader who was on his feet and moved to alert his team to be ready to move out as soon as they could.

Activity increased in a conference room as the teams met to make plans and finalize them. Bill leaned back against the wall for a moment, Andrew beside him.

"Jason is sure about this?" Andrew had no doubt that he was.

"He is. He has a patrol officer watching the building. His contact said that Lily and Loch had been moved around a lot from building to building. They were brought to this building really early this morning, under cover of darkness, they stated. I don't know who his contact is but I want to thank that person personally." Bill shoved away from the wall, heading for the parking lot and his vehicle, Jason at his side, search warrants in hand.

Standing near his vehicle, Bill eyed the building and then the officers moving into position. He nodded at the ETF lead who turned to his team and motioned them forward. Bill prayed that Lily and Loch were indeed in there and alive. He knew that God was in control of the situation.

The ETF men moved in, weapons at the ready. They searched each room before frowning at one another. They had not found the couple and that was strange.

Bill walked towards the ETF lead.

"John?"

"We can't find them. This is strange, Bill. If Jason's source was true and we have no reason to doubt that, they should be here. Are there any rooms that we need to know about that we haven't seen?"

Bill stared at him and then nodded. He was familiar with this building. It had been abandoned for more years than he could remember. As teens, he and his friends had explored it. John was not from the town.

"There is. God, please, let them be there." Bill ran for the walls at the back of the building and searched. His hands reached for a seemingly innocent panel and shoved violently at it. The panel slid to one side, revealing a dark and damp room behind it.

John's flashlight was out, shining around the room before it returned to a huddled pile of blankets. Bill was through the door and on his knees. John shouted for help before he was beside Bill, his hands helping to remove the blanket. Both men shared a look before Bill's hands were out to roll Loch onto his back. John reached for Lily, a hand feeling for a pulse.

The two men stood to one side as paramedics worked feverishly on the couple. Jason had approached and nodded as Bill spoke quietly. This was a crime scene now and once Lily and Loch were removed that would fall to Jason to lead the investigation.

The stretchers bearing Lily and Loch were rolled rapidly into the Emergency Department, medical staff waiting for them. Physicians ran to help, knowing that the couple's condition was unknown. All of the staff were aware of how long that the couple had been missing and would do what they could to treat them.

Bill watched closely, his phone in his hand for a moment. He prayed for a touch of healing from God for the two. It would take time he knew for them to be assessed and treatment started. He walked away to the outside, finding a quiet spot where he just stood, thinking through what had happened and then bending his head to pray.

"Luke?" Bill could hear the noise around Luke. "Can you talk?"

"I can. I'm just leaving a coffee shop. What can I do for you?" Luke almost held his breath, praying that his sister was found.

"Come to the hospital, Luke." Bill waited for Luke to process his words.

"Bill? I'm not sure that I understand. The hospital?" Luke's heart began to race, praying that his sister was safe.

"The hospital. We have Lily and Loch, Luke." Bill waited once more for Luke to respond.

“You have Lily? And Loch? Are they alive?” Luke threw his bag of food and cup of coffee into a nearby trashcan before he ran for his truck.

“They are, Luke. They’re not responding as yet but they’re in good hands.” Bill stared down at his phone before he felt a hand on his shoulder.

Andrew had appeared once he knew that Lily and Loch were safe and under care.

“Talk to me, Bill. Tell me what you found.”

“John’s team didn’t find them at first. We thought it was another dead-end. Then, I remembered roaming through the building with my friends when we were teens. There was a hidden room and that’s where they were. I don’t know that we would have found them if I hadn’t remembered that. God brought that memory back to me. That’s the only explanation that I can give.” Bill was sober as he spoke.

Andrew agreed. God had been at work there, he had no doubt. He had seen it too many times in the past to doubt Bill’s words. He walked back into the Emergency Department, looking for answers that were ready yet. He stood at Lily’s bedside, studying his friend and then walked to find Loch. Andrew’s thoughts were troubled. They had no way of knowing yet why they had disappeared or where they had been held.

Luke almost ran towards Bill, sliding to a halt with a hand out to the brick wall to stop his forward motion.

"Bill? What's the word? Where did you find them?" Luke's words tumbled over themselves as he tried to compose himself. He didn't realize that he had been weeping on the way, the tears leaving tracks down his cheeks.

"They're being assessed at the moment, Luke. We'll get you back as soon as we can. We found them in a hidden room in an abandoned building." Bill watched as Luke thought through his words.

"The Hooper building? We spent a lot of time there, looking for ghosts." Luke gave a brief grim smile. "The secret room?"

Bill nodded. Luke was familiar with the building, he knew. It had been a building that had attracted the teens over the years. God had protected Lily and Loch, that he was certain of.

Luke shifted on his feet, desperate to find his sister, but also afraid to do so. He didn't know if he wanted to find out what she had been through.

Chapter 27

His hand shaking as he reached out to touch Lily's hair, Luke blinked back tears. He felt that all he was doing at the moment was weeping. With his sister disappearing as she had, he had gone through the gamut of emotions. He was grateful that God had protected Lily and brought her back. Luke was just afraid of how this would affect her as a person and also in her career. Lily had always wanted to be a police officer and making detective had been a dream that she had not even imagined possible.

Lily's head twisted restlessly as she struggled to sleep. She had been awake long enough to talk with Jason although he had trouble following her train of thought. It was very disjointed and out of order, he thought. He would follow up with her once she was more alert and coherent.

Luke walked away at last, a dejected and discouraged slump to his shoulders. He paused as he saw Silas waiting for him just outside of the door.

"You could have come in, Silas." Luke stopped in front of his pastor.

"No, you needed that time with Lily. I'll go in later. She's sleeping?" Silas peered around Luke to study what he could see of Lily's bed.

"She is but she isn't." Luke scrubbed at his face. "She's not coherent when she does rouse. The physician said that was to be expected. It's just not

Lily. She has some of the clearest thinking processes that I know."

"She's been through a lot, Luke. And she's been in danger. People will shut down to some extent when that happens. I know that both Madigan and I were like that at some point during our adventure. I have counselled many people over the years who have faced trauma of some kind. Bill and Andrew felt the same."

"I have talked with them both. They were of a great help to me. I can't thank you enough for the prayers that you have offered over the last few days. They have helped. I often wonder how those who don't have faith get through things like this."

"They turn to crutches sometimes. Alcohol. Drugs. Depression with whatever comes with that. Marriage breakups. Suicides." Silas had seen it all in his time as a pastor. Many nights, he had fallen on his knees, broken in his own spirit because of what he was giving someone else.

"I guess that they have. How do I deal with the range of emotions that are going to come out?" Luke was thinking ahead, knowing that he had to be there for his sister. He just wasn't sure how Loch would fit into that picture.

"Loch will need counselling too. We'll all be there for them. Any of our friends will step in and pick up where they need to." Silas sat, a hand on Luke's shoulder as he sat as well. He began to pray for Luke and then for Lily and Loch.

Luke appreciated the caring and compassion from his group of friends and from his church family.

They had gathered around him in the last few days. He began to weep once more, his emotions raw.

Bill had been approaching the two men and paused as he heard Silas praying. He found the seat next to Luke, an arm across his friend's shoulders. He picked up the prayer as Silas finished. Jason has been with and headed for Loch's room. He turned as he found the doorway, his eyes on Luke.

Loch was still unconscious, a fact that was beginning tp worry the physicians. They felt that he should be awakening and wasn't. Jason stood for a moment, not sure why he was there when Loch was still unconscious but knew that he was praying that Loch would awaken and awaken right then and be coherent and alert.

Lily roused more fully in the middle of the night. She snuggled down under the blankets, feeling warm and cared for. She didn't understand that. As far as she knew, they were still captives. And that had not gone well. Lily was worried about Loch. He had taken the brunt of what they had been treated to. That had scared her more than she had been scared. She had been beaten as well.

Luke was on his feet as his sister's eyes opened, a hand reaching for hers. He felt her jump before she looked at him, her eyes huge with fear.

"Luke? Do they have you too?" Lily was worried about him.

"No, you're free, Lily. The team found you yesterday. Loch is safe as well." His thumb went out to flick away the tears that Lily could not control. "You're safe, Lily. You're safe."

"I am? Where are they? They wouldn't have let us go. They told us that we couldn't leave." Lily's eyes closed and she slept once more.

Luke found his chair once more, leaning back as he thought through what Lily had stated. He feared even more for his sister and Loch, knowing that they were still in grave danger. He knew who owned the building where they were found. Luke didn't know where that person was but he was determined to track him down and help bring him to justice.

Jason walked through the quiet hallways a few hours later. He was hoping that Lily or Loch was awake and could tell them what happened. He needed that information to move the case forward. There hadn't been anything concrete in what was retired by the crime lab the day before in the building. That had not surprised any of them. Whoever this was? They were being very careful to hide their evidence.

Lily roused as she heard quiet voices in her hospital room. She laid still, her eyes closed as she processed the words. Luke, she thought, and who else? Then, she realized it was a lady who she didn't know. Her eyes cracked open slightly.

"Emma? What do we do?" Luke's voice held desperation. "How do we keep Lily safe? She's out there on the front lines and vulnerable. I can't lose my sister. These last few days have been hard enough."

"I understand, Luke, to some extent how hard it can be. I thought that I had lost Abe in an accident and thought that for ten years. He thought that I didn't want him any more and had regretted our marriage. We were kept apart for that long. That being said, all I can say is be there for your sister. Leave her in God's hands as difficult as that can be. He has the best in mind for all of us, even though we doubt and question Him about that. Even now, Abe and I still question the path that we walked. If we had not done so, I would not have started my work and helped so very many people. Abe too has helped so many with his security team." Emma bit at her lip for a moment. "I understand your concern. Abe was like with his sister, Rebecca. She lost her first husband when they had been married for only three months. It was a murder. Rebecca also had a stalker that no one knew about except their uncle and he would not speak without her permission. That changed with Gideon moved in on her and married her quickly."

Luke had not taken his eyes from Emma until he saw a slight movement from Lily. He was on his feet, bending over his sister, a question on his lips that died as he saw her eyes on him. He could not and would not ask her what she had been through. He could see it in her eyes.

Emma watched Lily closely before she began to pray for her. She prayed for peace and a touch of the garment for this young lady so near in age to herself.

Chapter 28

Lily continued to rouse, hearing Luke calling her. She sighed to herself. She didn't want to wake up. She preferred the dimness of sleep where she didn't have to remember what had happened.

"Luke? Are you captive too?"

Luke gave a grim smile as he gripped his sister's hand tighter. God would have to work through this, he knew. And only God could bring the healing that she needed.

"No, I'm not, Lily. You're in the hospital. Don't say anything. Jason will be back around to get your statement." Luke turned to Emma, who shrugged. He didn't know when Jason would return, just that he would.

"I am." Lily shoved at the blankets and sat up, not waiting for Luke to raise the head of the bed. She frowned at Emma. "Who are you?" Lily didn't recognize Emma at first.

"I'm Emma Finlay. Loch is a friend. I've come to see what I can do for you." Emma gave a gentle smile, knowing that this would be a surprise for Lily.

"He's talked about you. Apparently, you're a whiz at finding people and information." Lily continued to frown, a headache hovering behind her eyes.

“He has? And that’s what people tell me. I do my best with the talents and gifts that God has given me.”

“Is that how you look at it? That’s a good way to do so.” Lily looked around, rousing more than she had been. “Luke? How’s Loch?”

“Loch? As far as I know, he’s still unconscious. They couldn’t get him to rouse yesterday.” Luke stared at his sister before he walked to the cupboard and returned with a bag of clothes. “Here. Get dressed and I’ll take you to him.” Luke walked away, leaving Emma staring at the door and then back at Lily.

“Need some help?” Emma reached to help Lily dress. She grimaced at the bruising on Lily’s body, giving evidence that Lily had been beaten at some point. Emma drew in a deep breath, wanting to talk to Lily about them but knowing that she could not. The investigators here needed to talk to her first. Emma’s arm was linked with Lily as Lily shuffled towards the door, pain on her face. “Lily?”

“I’m okay, Emma. I just hurt all over.” Lily’s hand went up to tuck her hair behind her ear, letting Emma get a glimpse of a ring on her left hand.

Emma frowned at that. Lily was not married, not that she was aware of. Her eyes raised to find Jason waiting just outside of the door, his eyes on Lily. He frowned as he saw the slow way in which Lily was moving. This was not her.

“Lily?” Jason’s voice cut through the pain that Lily was feeling.

Lily looked up at Jason, squinting to study him.

"Jason? You need to talk with me?" Lily sighed. She wanted to find Loch but Jason would need to take her statement first.

"I do, Lily." Jason's hand went out to help steady her. "Here, let's sit in this quiet corner." He nodded at Emma to stay. "Talk to me, Lily. Then, we'll get you in to see Loch." He too caught the movement of Lily's hand and then the glint of the ring on her finger. He frowned at that. What was going on? He had no idea but he prayed that he would find out soon.

Lily sank down into a chair gratefully, grasping at Emma's hand. She refused to let go of it. She didn't see Luke watching from a nearby chair, his eyes intent on her. Lily didn't know where to start.

"Where do I start, Jason?" Lily drew in a deep breath. She didn't want to relive what had happened. It had terrified her, to say the least, and she knew that reliving it would deepen her fear. Lily was also afraid for Loch and needed to see him. Jason would allow that, she knew, once her statement had been given.

"We know that you were in Mistletoe that day, Lily. I went back there and confirmed that. Now, we know that you were taken from the side of the highway. We found your jacket. Loch's car was returned to his home. That set off a lot of searching, Lily, without any answers." Jason looked down at his notebook that he held in his hand. "Just start where it all began."

Lily nodded, drawing in a deep breath. Her heart whispered a prayer for peace and strength to get through the memories of the events that had shut her down.

Lily's thoughts drifted back to that Saturday. Loch and she had wandered Mistletoe, finding that their likes and dislikes were more in tune than they remembered. She had been happy, she knew, as had been Loch. They had started their travel home, not realizing how closely that they had been followed all that day.

Loch had not been that aware of the traffic around him. He didn't see the trucks moving in around him until Lily gave an exclamation. He shot her a look before he looked in horror at the truck that was slamming on its brakes right in front of him. Loch could not move to pass him due to the truck beside him. A quick glance in his rearview mirror showed a truck tight behind him. The truck to his side turned into him. Loch spun his wheel and headed for the grass on the side of the road, bumping to a stop. Lily's head was moving rapidly, trying to find a way out for them. Only there wasn't one. Men with drawn weapons appeared around the vehicle.

Loch's hands raised as he shared a quick look with Lily. Their doors were forced open and both of them were pulled from the vehicle. Loch stumbled to keep to his feet as he watched Lily's jacket pulled from her and dropped on the trampled grass. The couple were shoved forward and then into separate trucks. Loch fought this, twisting and turning under the hands that held him in a tight grip.

Lily struggled to escape as well. Shoved into the truck, a hand was clamped tight on her wrist, preventing her from escaping. She watched as the trucks pulled away, frowning as Loch's vehicle tucked inbetween the trucks. Lily jumped as a blindfold was dropped over her eyes. This was not good, she knew. She had no idea who the men were or where they were heading. Lily was afraid, deeply afraid, to the point that she could not pray. She knew that God was still there and that the Holy Spirit was praying for her.

Chapter 29

Lily felt the truck slowing and then making a number of turns. She was unable to keep track of how many that there were. The truck slowed once more and then stopped. Lily waited for the man beside her to move but he didn't. She waited, praying all the time that this was just a sick nightmare but she knew that it was not.

Pulled from the truck at last, Lily stumbled as she tried to regain her balance. She was pulled roughly over uneven ground and then into a building. She listened carefully and heard Loch behind her. She was thankful that he was there. Now, she had to figure out who had kidnapped them and why.

Lily's hands hit the wall in front of her, bringing a small sound of pain from her. She could hear Loch's protests from beside her. She turned so that her back was to the wall. Loch's arm brushed against her and she felt him reach for her hand. Hers gripped his tightly as they waited for what, they weren't sure about.

Loch's head tilted as he listened. He could hear the noise about them, the quiet conversation that he could not understand, and then felt Lily's hand gripping his. He had no idea who the men were. They had kept their faces covered with sunglasses and masks. Loch was deeply afraid for Lily. They had managed to stay safe. Loch regretted their decision to head to Mistletoe on their own even though it had been a wonderful day.

The men milled around in front of the couple, stepping over the debris on the floor. The building was decrepit and old, with many gaps in the walls and broken windows. The room that they were in was an inside room and still in good shape. There was no way to escape other than the door that they stood in front of. A rudimentary washroom had been built at some point and still worked. This was where the plan was to keep Loch and Lily for now.

The door squeaked closed behind the men at last, leaving Loch and Lily still standing, hand in hand, against the wall opposite the door. The couple waited for someone to speak before Lily was pulling off her blindfold. She blinked rapidly before she was searching for a way out and not finding one, then searching for anything that she could use for a weapon. She could find nothing.

Loch stared at her and then made his own search. He stood with a hand planted flat against the door, lost in thought.

"Lily? Did you recognize the men or the trucks?"

Lily shook her head. She hadn't. She felt her pocket. It was as she thought. Her phone had disappeared at some point.

"Do you have your phone?"

Loch felt his pockets and shook his head. They had both not felt their phones being removed from their pockets. They stared at one another, dismay in their looks that this had happened.

Reaching to wrap Lily into a hug, Loch held on to her. He could feel her shudder under the burden of her emotions. He dropped a kiss on the top of her head.

Lily stood in the circle of Loch's arms, feeling his determination to protect her. She knew that would be extremely impossible to do. She didn't think that they would be given that chance. Lily glanced at her watch. It was now evening. Lily was waiting for the men to return. Only, they didn't, not until the morning. She curled up in a corner of the room where she could watch the door.

Loch took another corner, watching Lily. He shrugged out of his jacket, walked over to Lily, and draped it around her. He then returned to his corner, his head back against the wall. His eyes closed as he began to pray and beg God for release. Loch cracked his eyes slightly open to watch Lily. He sighed. How was he to get her away from this?

The night passed slowly. Lily would rise every once in a while and pace the room, trying the door each time even though she knew that it would be locked. She would turn and watch Loch, seeing that he was asleep. Lily finally slept towards morning, awakening to the rattling of the door as it opened.

The men stood for a moment and studied the couple before moving in on them and dragging them to their feet. Lily and Loch stood, their arms locked in strong grips. Loch drew in a deep breath. He had no idea what was coming but he was afraid. Lily kept her face neutral despite her thoughts racing. She didn't like what she thought was coming and she too prayed for peace in the situation.

The leader of the men stared at Loch and then at Lily. He had his orders. His orders didn't bother him. It would not be the first time that he had beaten a woman and it really didn't matter to him that Lily was an officer. He nodded at the men holding Loch. Loch was dragged backwards and slammed into the wall. His eyes closed for a moment against the pain that he felt. He looked up against, his eyes half-closed as he heard Lily's voice. Loch could not make out her words but she sounded angry.

A yell of rage exploded from Loch as his body twisted and turned in his struggle to free himself. It didn't work. He continued to yell, his rage and fear for Lily grew as he watched the fists that hammered into her.

Lily felt the first blow to her face as her head flew to the side. This is not what she had expected but she should have. Fists continued to pound into her before she slumped, only held upright by the hands of the men who had her in their grip.

The leader walked towards Loch, a hand out to slam Loch's head against the wall. Loch waited for the pain to ease and his vision to clear.

"Marry her or she dies." The men walked away, Loch dropping to the ground in pain from the blows that he had taken.

Loch didn't rouse for a while. He struggled at last to sit up, his arms wrapping around his abdomen. His head dropped for a moment as he struggled to understand what had happened. His head raised once more as his vision cleared. Loch searched for Lily, not seeing her at first. His vision dropped to the floor and he saw the crumpled heap that was Lily.

A strangled cry rose from him before he was crawling towards her. A shaking hand reached out to touch her before he gathered her into his arms. Sitting crosslegged on the floor, he held her, a hand brushing back the hair from her face. Lily roused slightly before she groaned and was lost to him again.

Loch struggled with his emotions, sobs rising within him. He hurt because his lady hurt. Yes, he had finally admitted to himself that she was the love of his life.

Lily roused at last, feeling arms tight around her. She groaned again, not realizing that hers were the groans that she heard. She felt herself being shifted in someone's arm and her head went down on a shoulder. She had no idea what had happened but she hurt and hurt badly.

Chapter 30

Loch laid Lily down carefully before he stumbled to his feet and to the washroom. He tore off a sleeve of his shirt and soaked it in water. The water was cold but that would have to do. He was back on his knees beside his lady, wiping at her face. He felt her shifting under his touch and that worried him. Loch felt along her abdomen and ribs, finding her moving away even from his light touch. That worried him.

Lily struggled to sit up, Loch's arm around her to stabilize her. She looked around through blurry eyes, not sure what had happened.

"Loch?" Lily's voice was barely audible. "What happened?"

"They beat you, Lily. I couldn't get loose to help you." Loch was almost in tears as he remembered that beating and his inability to get to his lady.

"They did? Why?"

"I don't know, Lily. I don't know." Something was niggling at Loch's memory. He just couldn't remember it.

"It doesn't make sense, Loch." Lily leaned against him, unable to sit upright. "I need to lie down." Lily slept and didn't know that Loch had carried her to a wall that he could lean against and hold her wrapped in his arms.

Early morning found Loch roused by a savage kick to his leg. He struggled to awaken and stared around at the group of men who stood around them once more.

Lily roused as well, staring up at the men before she was dragged to her feet and then across the room from Loch. Loch was forcibly restrained against the wall. He struggled to escape but was unable to release himself from the hands.

The leader stared at Loch, a hard and angry look on his face. He nodded at the man standing in front of Lily. Lily's beating began again despite the angry and frantic shouts from Loch. Lily slumped to the floor once more, unconscious. Loch stared at her in shock before he was slammed back against the wall once more. He dropped to the floor, hearing the door lock behind the men. Loch crawled towards Lily, a hand out to touch her. This time, he didn't gather her up into his arms. Instead, he lay beside her and gathered her close. He slept, not hearing the door open and a bag containing food dropped to the floor.

This went on for a few days, Lily threatened with a beating until finally Loch nodded. He had to agree to their demands. If he didn't, then Lily would be killed. Of that he was certain. Lily and Loch were dragged to their feet and shoved across the rough and broken floor to trucks. They were shoved into different trucks once more and the trucks drove away.

Forced to sign an application, Lily slumped against the seat back. She was barely aware of what was happening at the moment but her mind was starting to clear. She was afraid for Loch, knowing that he would agree to their demands. And it wasn't fair. Her life was not worth that, Lily decided. She was not aware that she was the love of Loch's life and he would do anything to protect her and save her.

Loch stared out of the truck window. They were on the move again, this time to another town. He shifted to stare behind him, knowing that the truck following them carried Lily. He watched as the trucks pulled into a nearby town, a small town that he had never come to previously.

Dropping to the ground, Loch reached for Lily's hand. He was not prepared for this next step, he knew, but he also realized that they had no choice. Lily would be dead if they didn't. Forced to walk into a building, Loch's hand tightened on Lily's, standing as close to her as he could.

Lily stared around, worry and fear working through her. She had to agree with Loch's whispered words. This was not how she had expected to have this day happen.

The minister who appeared in the room watched the younger couple with a hard look on his face. This was not the first time that he had done this. He was paid well for his time. He didn't care why they were being forced to marry. That was none of his business. A quick ceremony followed his appearance before he pocketed the bills that he was handed and disappeared.

Lily leaned against Loch, struggling with her emotions. She was in pain and distress and knew that Loch was as well. She turned her face up to him, finding him watching her. His arm was now around her and it tightened as he tried to express his emotions to her.

They were forced back into separate trucks. Lily once more huddled into a corner, not looking around at the men with her. Her focus was on the gold ring that now encircled her finger. She was angry at how that had happened. Neither she nor Loch had had any say in how it happened. Her beatings had left Loch feeling as if he had had no choice.

Shoved into another room in another decrepit and broken building, Lily had swayed on her feet, fatigue and pain clouding her mind. Loch stood away from her, watching as a bag of food was dropped to the floor before the door was slammed shut and locked once more. He was across the room, catching Lily as her body dropped towards the floor. Her head hit his shoulder as her eyes closed.

Loch was distraught, to say the least. He looked up, begging God to free them. He needed to get his lady to medical help and soon. He too slept, Lily held in his arms. They didn't hear the door unlock and open once more as the leader of the men stood there with a frown on his face. That man needed to talk with them. Only, that was not happening at the moment. He walked away, two men left behind to guard the captives.

Days passed like this. The couple were moved once more to another building, the door locking behind them as their bodies were just dumped to the floor. The men didn't care about the debris on the floor. A rough and dirty blanket was dropped over them. Other than that, there was no comfort left for them. The door was locked behind them once more.

The leader stood and stared at the building. He had not been able to interrogate the couple any further. They just had not roused enough for him to do that. And he had to do that. If he didn't and couldn't obtain their further cooperation, they would be left there to die. Not that it mattered much to him. He was paid whether or not they cooperated with him.

The sun sank below the horizon, sending out its rosy and purplish rays. The light reflected on the remaining dirty window panes of the building. Darkness dropped on the town and coldness dropped as well. With the coldness, Loch moved closer to Lily, wrapping her into his arms and pulling the dirty blanket up over them. He was not aware that was what he was doing. He did it instinctively.

Chapter 31

The shouts and hammering at the doors sounded loudly as the Emergency Task Force moved through the building. They stopped at the locked door before hammering at it and knocking it open. The door flew back against the wall, slamming into it with a loud thud.

Jason was through the door behind the men, then stared around. A sudden yell had him spinning before he was across the room and on his knees. Calls went out for the paramedics.

Jason and the other officers stepped to one side as the paramedics moved in and began their assessments. Quickly starting the IV lines and then transferring the couple to their stretchers, the stretchers were then rolled across the rough floor and pavement. They were quickly loaded into the paramedic rigs and driven away.

Lily came back to the present, her right hand rubbing at her left hand. There had been some minor fractures of that hand and it was hurting. Her fingers lingered on the ring that Loch had placed there. They had not had any chance to talk. Lily prayed that Loch would be receptive to what had happened.

Jason was watching Lily closely, seeing the stress and pain that covered Lily's face. He studied his notes.

"Lily? Can you describe the men?"

Lily shook her head. She had not gotten that good of a look at them at first and after the beatings, she was in no condition to remember them.

"I'm sorry, Jason. I don't. They were well hidden behind disguises at the first. After the beatings, I was in too much pain and stress to see them. Loch might have a better picture than I do." Lily sighed. "I hate this, Jason. This should not have happened." She held up her left hand, the ring glinting in the light.

"No, it shouldn't have, Lily. And you have no idea why?" Jason waited for her to shake her head. "We heard nothing about this on the street. And that is unusual."

"It is." Lily was on her feet, not excusing herself, an arm wrapped around herself. She stumbled as she walked away, heading for Loch. She stood in his hospital room doorway for a moment, composing herself. Tears were near the surface, tears of all ilks, but mostly for Loch. He had been hurt because of her and that she had trouble dealing with. All she could do was turn that over to God and let Him work it out. He had a plan and purpose for this even though they could not see it at present.

Standing at Loch's beside, Lily studied the man who was now her groom. She wasn't sure why but she would do everything that she could to protect him. And now that he was family, her fellow officers would do the same. That went without saying. The police force in Elmton was a close group, now that the bad ones had been weeded out. That was a story in itself, pertinent to one of her friends.

Her hand reached to touch his cheek, feeling the whiskers rough under her fingers. This was not him, she knew. He liked to be clean-shaven. That was one of the issues that had risen lately with their abduction.

Loch moved restlessly before his body stilled. He felt Lily's hand on his face and turned into it. Without opening his eyes, he spoke to his bride, sure that it was her that had touched him.

"Lily? Are you okay?"

"I am, Loch. And so are you. We're in the hospital. Someone found us and got us out." Lily was puzzled by that. She knew that they had been moved from building to building and from town to town. She didn't understand why. "Jason's here. He needs to talk with you."

"He does?" Loch groaned as he shoved himself up on the pillows, feeling the head of the bed raising as Lily found the button to do that. His eyes opened and closed as he blinked to clear his vision. "Lily? Did that really happen?" Loch watched her with concern but also love for her in his eyes.

Lily studied him with a frown on her face. She felt that was all she was doing lately, frowning at someone or something.

"It did." Her finger lightly touched the wedding band on his finger. "I don't know why though."

"There's a reason there and it involves both of us. I'm not sure why." Loch sighed, feeling at his ribs and abdomen. "Is anything broken?"

"Not for you. I have some fractures in my hand." Lily stared at him for a moment, not realizing that her emotions and love for Loch were evident on her face. "I don't get why, Loch. I know. I'm repeating myself. And I will until I understand it."

"Me as well." Loch reached to hug her, holding on as he felt the tears that she would not shed causing her body to shudder. "It's okay, Lily. We'll get this figured out. When can we leave?"

"Today, I think. Jason wants your statement before we do." Lily was sober. "Where do we live, Loch? We're married now, whether or not that's what we wanted."

"We'll figure it out. For today, I'll grab some stuff from my home and head for yours. Where's Luke?" Loch looked around her as he heard footsteps and Luke appeared. "Luke?"

Luke's hand went up to silence the other man, the man who was now family. Luke didn't understand how that had happened, but it had. Now, they had to work to figure that out. Emma has spoken with him and left a pile of information for him. That same information had been handed to Jason.

"Jason wants to speak with you, Loch, when you're ready. Lily? I'll be in the waiting room." Luke hesitated, wanting to say more but walked away, praying for his sister and her now groom.

Jason laid a hand on Luke's shoulder as he passed him, pausing as well in the room doorway. He nodded as Lily walked towards him before he gave her a hug, whispered a prayer in her ear, and sent her to find Luke. His attention went to Loch, finding Loch now sitting on the side of the bed.

"Loch?" Jason sat in front of him, his notebook out on the table. "Talk to me. Help me to understand what happened."

Loch shrugged, yawning before he rubbed at his cheek. He hated the way he looked. He knew that Lily didn't mind but that was not how he wanted to appear before her. Loch began to pray, begging God to save his lady. It didn't matter about him, he said, but Lily needed to be safe. And he didn't know how to do that.

"Okay, Jason. Let me tell you what happened." Loch did just that, his words almost identical to Lily's except he could not understand why Lily had been beaten as she had.

"There's a reason for that, Loch, and we need to find out why. They targeted you two. We just don't understand why. Maybe what Emma left will help."

Loch looked at him in surprise and then nodded. Yes, Emma would have been around. She had been a friend of his while he lived in Riverville.

"Has Abe's team shown up yet?" Loch gave a brief smile. "Or are they leaving our security to Richard?"

"Both of them and also Don from Oak City are weighing in. I would not be surprised to see them rotating around with you two. Lily's not going to be working for a while." Jason didn't say his fears, that Lily would decide that she could no longer do the work of an investigator and resign. That had happened before.

Chapter 32

Jason walked back through the department, fatigue weighing him down as did the worry for Lily and Loch. He paused at Bill's door and then searched for Andrew. He stood for a moment watching Andrew before that man looked up and waved him in.

"Jason? You look as if you are carrying the weight of the world." Andrew was worried about Jason, knowing how hard he had been working to find Lily and Loch.

"I guess that I am, Andrew. I have Lily and Loch's statements. It's not making sense. Loch said that Lily was beaten until he agreed to marry her." Jason caught the look of shock on the police chief's face. "I don't understand why."

Andrew had been informed that the couple had married but not the circumstances surrounding it.

"And what is your feeling about this?" Andrew waited patiently for Jason to compose himself and then waited for him to think through what he knew.

"I don't know what to think, Andrew. Loch and Lily are heading for her home. She's not saying much, which is unusual for her. Given what she went through, I can understand that. I know how it was with Julia." Jason rose and walked away, leaving Andrew staring after him.

Andrew nodded before his attention went back to the reports on his desk. He read for a while before he was on his feet, heading for his car and then heading for Lily. He needed to speak with her in person.

Luke stood back from the door to allow Andrew to enter. He had been on his way out, needing to get to work when Andrew appeared. There was soft conversation in the kitchen, Phoebe, Madigan, and Silas appearing.

"How are they?" Andrew kept his voice soft.

Luke shrugged, not sure how his sister was.

"I don't know, Andrew. Maybe you can read her better than I can. She's shutting down just to protect herself and to protect Loch." Luke walked away, leaving Andrew to head for the kitchen.

Lily turned as she heard new footsteps, fear momentarily crossing her face. Her face relaxed as she recognized Andrew.

"Andrew? You're here?" Lily accepted the hug from a friend and then stepped backwards, hitting Loch who stood behind her. His arms were wrapped around her, making her feel safe for a moment.

"I am, Lily. I need to see you and speak with you two." Andrew shared a look with Phoebe before he pointed to the table. "It looks as if I walked in on a meal."

"You did, Drew." Phoebe continued to fill the soup bowls and hand them to Madigan. Silas was moving around finding beverages for them all. "Sit. We'll eat and then we'll pray. These two need that."

An hour later, Andrew raised his head, glancing at the clock on the stove. He needed to be back in the office shortly. But he did want to speak with these two.

"Lily? Loch? What can we do for you two?" Andre waited patiently as the couple shared a look.

"I don't know that anyone can do anything for us, Andrew." Loch drew in a deep breath. "We need to find the men or women responsible for this. And I gather that you don't have enough information to do that or you would have already. Lily didn't deserve to be beaten as she saw. Neither one of us deserved to be forced into marriage." Loch's voice had grown sterner and graver with each word. He was more than a little worried about Lily. He had seen the change in her over the morning and that worried him not a little bit.

"We are doing what we can to protect you two." Andrew rose, tidying away his dishes. "Call me, Lily. I want to talk to you tomorrow or the next day. For now, get what rest you can. And trust God that He has you in His care."

Lily nodded, not really believing that any more. The situation that she had just been rescued from had shaken her faith to the core. She knew that she needed to work through that but it was hard. She was ready to walk away from her church and her faith. Lily knew that she couldn't but the temptation to do so was growing stronger every hour.

Loch dropped his head. The exhaustion that had been plaguing him in the hospital had grown stronger. Silas was on his feet, a hand out to draw Loch to his feet and then with a hand to Loch's back, he directed him down the hall to a spare bedroom. Loch nodded with gratitude as he dropped down on the bed, pulling a blanket over himself. He didn't hear Silas walk away and close the door quietly behind him. Silas stood for a moment, staring at the floor, unable to frame a prayer for the couple.

Lily paced her home late that afternoon. She was alone for the moment, as alone as she could be with Loch sleeping in a room down the hall. She would pause in front of it, a hand out to touch the door, before she would walk away. Lily wanted Loch to wake up and talk with her. She needed him to comfort her and tell her that God was in control.

Loch rose at last, squinting at the clock. He sighed. He had not planned on sleeping that long. He struggled to his feet and headed to find Lily. He stood and watched as she slept, curled up on the couch. Loch draped a blanket over her, a hand resting on her hair before he dropped a kiss on her cheek. He watched with a sad smile as she smiled in her sleep and snuggled down under the covers.

Turning away from Lily, Loch studied her home. He liked the decor and colourings that she had chosen. She had taken a house and made it into a home that was both restful and welcoming.

He headed for the kitchen, not that he was hungry but he needed something to drink. He paused as he heard a slight noise. Luke appeared from the kitchen, startling Loch. He drew in a deep breath. He was jumping at everything, Loch knew, and that was not him.

"Loch? You were asleep when I got here. Are you feeling any better?" Luke studied the man who was now his brother-in-law.

"Not really. I'm sorry, Luke. I couldn't stop them. I tried." Loch drew in a deep breath, not sure what to say.

"I understand, Loch. I know that you would try to do what you could to protect her. They were just too much for you." Luke rubbed at his face. He really didn't know what to say. He had heard their story and had been shocked at the men's demands.

"I don't either, Luke. They gave no reason for demanding that. They would have continued to beat her until they killed her. I couldn't let that happen." Loch's voice was shuddering from his strong emotions. "This is not how she should have married. She deserved much better."

"I understand, Loch." Luke repeated his words. He didn't continue. If he had, he would have told Loch that he was exactly who Lily needed in her life and always had been.

Chapter 33

Lily was on her feet in the early morning, almost running for her office. She dug through the paperwork and files that littered the top of her desk, frowning at the mess. This was not her. Lily was neat and kept her desk neat. She sat, opening the file that she had dug up. A frown appeared on her face as she did so. She cradled her left hand in her right hand as she read.

A slight noise had Lily jumping and staring around in fear. She rose, heading for the window in the office, pulling the drape to one side to peer outside. It was as she had expected. There were men out there, men who shouldn't be there. She reached for the phone that was in her pocket, calling for help.

An arm around her caused a small scream to issue from Lily. She twisted to see Loch standing with her, watching the outside as well.

"Lily? Who are they?" Loch kept his voice low.

"I don't know. They look familiar. I think they are some of our captors. I called it in." Lily's voice was low as well as she waited for help.

Police officers moved in, stopping the men from leaving. The men struggled to escape and were taken to the ground and handcuffed. Pulled to their feet, they were shoved around the house and then into patrol vehicles.

Jason approached the house, finding Lily unlocking the back door and cracking it open enough to let him slip inside.

"Jason? Who were they?" Lily's voice was still quiet and subdued.

"We don't know. Do you recognize them?"

"We think that they were some of our abductors. At least, that's what Lily thinks. I just don't remember them all that well."

"They are, Jason, With this arrest, maybe this will be over." Lily was hopeful but doubted that her wish would come true.

"We'll do what we can, Lily. You know that." Jason finally walked away from them, not sure that he had accomplished anything in interviewing them. They just weren't sure enough of the men to say for certain that they were their abductors.

Lily turned to Loch, finding him just reaching to sweep her into a hug. She held onto him, finding comfort in his arms. Leaning back after a while, she looked up at him, finding him standing with his eyes closed.

"Loch? Do you need to go to your studio?"

"I do, Lily. I do. I haven't been there for a few days and I need to get a sense of what is waiting for me. Come with me. You're not working for now." Loch tugged her with him, watching as she handed him her keys. "You're sure?"

"I am, Loch. I'm sure." Lily didn't look at him, not wanting him to see the emotions that were raw and open on her face.

Loch studied her and then studied the area around them. He was not comfortable driving away from her home, sensing the danger that was gathering around them. He sighed, turning his head as he heard a car pulling to a stop behind Lily's car. Loch frowned at the man who was approaching them.

"Lily? Do you know this man?" Loch nodded towards him. Loch, in a fog from his adventure, didn't recognize Abe Finlay, a friend from Riverville.

Lily looked out of the window and then was out of the car, moving into the man's hug.

"Abe? What are you doing here? And how many of your team are here?"

Abe Finlay grinned at her. He had been in touch with Jason and felt compelled to head that way.

"Just Matt, Ian, and Murphy. We're here for the day. Now, where are you heading?" Abe watched as Loch approached.

Loch sighed. He hadn't recognized Abe and that concerned him.

"Abe?"

"Head for our vehicle, Loch. We're with you today." Abe's voice, although kindly, was stern. He didn't wait for Loch or Lily to protest but turned them that way and walked after them, his head turning as he searched the area around the house. He could feel the danger and the eyes that were watching them.

Loch moved through his studio, working away as best that he could. He knew that Lily was working away in the office, sorting through the accumulated mail and requests for photo sessions. He turned as Murphy approached him.

"Murphy? What's on your mind?" Loch grinned at the man for a moment before he sobered.

"I'm worried about you and Lily, Loch. Lily told us what happened. You're not talking about it."

Loch shook his head. He wasn't talking about it and should, he knew. He studied his friend and then sighed.

"Come on back to the kitchen, Murphy. We do need to talk. I need some advice from someone just like you."

Murphy listened as Loch poured out all his feelings and fears. Ian stood outside of the kitchen, listening. He knew that Loch would not mind that. Abe approached finally, pulling Ian away, intent on coming up with a solution to protect the two.

"Ian?" Abe glanced towards the kitchen and then at Lily who was standing beside him. "Lil?"

"I know. Loch is talking to Murphy and he needs to do that. Don't worry. I'm talking to someone as well." Lily sighed, her hand rubbing at the bandage on her other hand. "I don't understand why, though. We're not getting the packages and letters and threats that should be coming at us."

"Whoever this is has read you correctly, Lily. They know those kinds of things won't work with you. And because Loch is with you, they won't work on him either. They are someone likely who has been close to you." Ian sighed. This is not how the day was to have been. They had gone over Loch's security system and updated it as much as they could. Now, they were facing the couple and what they could do for them. And that would not be a lot, Ian knew from experience.

Lily nodded. That was the consensus that both she and Loch had come to. They were going back over their friends and acquaintances from school days and forward. Loch had provided a list for her that she was comparing to hers.

"We're working through a list of people who we know. I've sent it on to Emma, Abe." Lily was disturbed. How did they do this? How did they stay safe and find the ones responsible? No one could give them any idea of how to do that other than the obvious. Lily walked away, heading for the front door and stepped outside, needing to be alone. She didn't know that Matt had followed her and stood beside her.

Chapter 34

Matt watched the traffic passing them, both vehicular and pedestrian. His eyes narrowed as he watched the youth standing in front of a building across from them. The youth was watching Lily closely. Matt touched Lily's arm causing her to jump.

"Lily? Do you know that youth across there?" Matt nodded at him.

Lily's eyes narrowed as she searched for the youth and then she too nodded.

"I do, Matt. He's from the youth group at the church even though he lives on the street. He wants something." Lily made a move to step away from Loch's building, frowning at Matt as he prevented her from doing that.

"I get that you trust him, Lily, but don't walk over there. Let him come to you. They may be waiting for you to do just that to nab you again." Matt's hand turned Lily back into the building before he walked casually across the street and stood beside the youth. He stared into the store window, not really intent on what was in it. He waited for the youth to speak.

"You a friend of Lily's?"

Matt had to strain to hear the words.

"I am. And you are too. What do you have for her?" Matt took the paper quickly proffered to him before he moved away to stare into another shop window. He tucked the paper away, knowing that he would give it to Lily. He feared for his friend and her groom. He knew how quickly things could change. That had happened to him and his wife, Sarah.

The youth sauntered away, seemingly without a destination in mind. Once he was out of sight of Matt, he began to run, heading for the church and Silas. He needed to talk to Silas, who would help him. He was afraid for his life, now that he had approached Lily in that way. The youth knew the man responsible and how vicious and deranged the man was.

Silas walked up to the youth, a hand out to draw him away from the street and to safety. He had no idea why he had felt led to approach the youth but he obeyed God's nudge. He shoved the youth into his car and disappeared, heading for his home. He knew that Madigan would have an idea of what to do.

Lily shivered, feeling cold even though it was not that cold out. Matt turned her back into the studio, his eyes on Abe as he stood just inside the door, waiting for them. He assessed Lily, seeing the fragility that she was becoming to display. He didn't like that but he had seen it before.

Loch walked towards Lily, drawing her into a hug and then turning her towards the stairs.

"Come on, sweetheart. I need to pack some more stuff to take to the house."

Loch followed her up the stairs to his apartment. Lilly stopped at the door, a hand reaching for it before she withdrew it. She could not bring herself to reach for it again.

A frown on his face, Loch reached around her, intent on opening the door. He stopped in shock as Lily's hand grasped his arm and pulled him back down the stairs, almost on a run.

The men waiting for them spun as they clattered back down the stairs. Ian and Matt were past them, heading for the stairs and up to the door. They shared a look before they felt around the door.

"Here, Ian." Matt withdrew his hand. "There's a piece of wire there. We need the bomb squad, I suspect."

Abe looked around as the two men appeared once more before his head tilted towards the front door. Matt headed that way as Ian headed for the back door. Murphy stood near Lily and Loch, a serious look on his face. Something had happened, he knew, and that meant more danger for the couple.

"Abe? We need to clear the building. I suspect that there's a bomb up there." Matt had his phone out to call for help. "Lily? Let's move you and Loch away from here."

Lily shook off her shock and then grabbed for Loch's hand, pulling him with her. The four men surrounded them, watchful for anyone who might mean Lily and Loch harm. This was a dangerous time for them, they knew.

Abe stood with his back against the vehicle door, watching the activity surrounding Loch's building. Bill had waved as he had arrived. The windows were lowered on the vehicle and he could hear the quiet conversation between Lily and Loch. His head tilted for a moment as he listened.

The other three of his team stood around nearby, not watching the activity across the street from them but what was happening around them. This was a time that they could be taken out and either be killed or disappear again. None of them could understand why they had been forced to marry.

"Abe?" Loch's voice had Abe turning away from the activity to face him. 'What are your thoughts? I know that Emma's working on it."

"She is. She was muttering early this morning about something. Why?" Abe waited for Loch to gather his thoughts and continue with his questions.

Loch hesitated, not sure how to express his thoughts. He struggled with that, fear for Lily uppermost in his mind.

"I don't understand why we were forced to marry. It's not as if we had been dating. Why?" Loch felt Lily's hand on his.

"That is a good question, Loch. I'm not sure that any of us understand it at all. I suspect that you both crossed paths with someone who wanted to harm you and chose this way. Neither of you believe in divorce and they knew that this would not be an option for you. Am I correct?" Abe watched them both nod in agreement. "So, by making you marry, they think that they have ruined your lives. The way that I am reading you two is that it won't."

Lily was nodding at Abe's words. She knew that she loved Loch and would be devastated if he decided to walk away from her. She wasn't sure how he felt. He had been hard to read over the last couple of days. Besides that, they had not had a chance to discuss what had happened.

Loch was in agreement with Abe's words as well. He was head over heels in love with Lily. He knew that they needed to talk. There just hadn't been time to talk about it.

Chapter 35

Loch's hand tightened on Lily's as he watched the activity around his building. He wanted to go back in but he couldn't. Not yet, anyway. He prayed for a quick resolution of the adventure that they were going through. That didn't seem to be happening. Loch was struggling to see God's hand in it all and just couldn't. He had talked with Luke about it and Luke had reassured him that God was there and was in control, even if he could not see or understand it.

Bill stood for a moment and stared at the bomb squad leader. He shook his head and then turned as he heard a heavy diesel motor as a fire ladder truck approached. The only way to enter the apartment without setting off the bomb was through the window. And to reach that they had decided to bring in a ladder truck and have firefighters on stand-by. Just in case. Bill nodded at him before he turned to find Murphy nearby.

"Bill?" Murphy glanced between Bill, the ladder truck, and the bomb squad leader who was walking away.

"They can't go in through the door. Whatever it was that stopped Loch and Lily? They would not have survived if they had opened that door." Bill was both frustrated and worried.

Murphy nodded. He had spoken with both Ian and Matt. Their experience had had them determining that very fact. Abe was aware of what their thoughts were.

"Who is after them, Bill? Do you have any idea?"

Bill shook his head, frustrated at that as well.

"We don't. There is nothing in either one of their pasts to show anyone who would want them harm. Sure, Lily has had threats against her over her years as an officer but none of them seem to be in play here." Bill squinted at Murphy. "What are you thinking?" He looked past Murphy to see Richard approaching. "Richard?"

"Bill. Murphy. Luke called me. He was heading out of town but wanted someone with these two. We're making arrangements to do that. I'm working it out with Abe." Richard stood with his back to the building, his keen eyes searching the area. He knew that his four team members were around in the crowd that had gathered, just waiting for anyone who seemed out of place.

"Richard? What are your thoughts?" Murphy waited patiently for Richard to respond.

"My thoughts? That there is someone in town with a hate on for both Lily and Loch. They want to destroy them and their reputations. Making them marry like this? It would make it seem as if they were not living up to their Christian beliefs. This could be used to drag them down if someone really wanted to." Richard mulled through his thoughts. "I wish I knew who it was behind all this. I don't even know if it's someone from this town or another town."

Bill stared at him first in shock and then in horror. He had not even considered that scenario.

Murphy was nodding. Given that Loch had lived in Riverville, that was a definite possibility. Riverville was not really that far from Elmton.

"Are you serious, Richard? Bill paced away and then came back. "Why would you say that?"

"You're not finding anyone here who is obvious or not so obvious." Richard nodded towards where Loch had exited the vehicle and stood leaning against it. "There may be someone in Riverville who hates him enough to do this."

Bill nodded. He would need to reach out to Frankie Brennan, a detective on the Riverville force, who he had worked with in past cases. He walked away from the two security team men and headed for his car. He sat inside, the door open, before he reached for his phone. He had to leave a voice mail for Frankie but Bill knew that Frankie would call him back when he was able to.

Lily was out of the vehicle and at Bill's car before anyone could stop her. She had a look of absolute fear on her face. Her phone was almost tossed at Bill, who caught it with a frown on his face.

"Lily?" Bill was out of his vehicle, a hand on Lily's arm moving her back towards the security men.

"Bill? Who is this?" Lily pointed a shaking finger at her phone. "Read that. Someone has my work cell number."

"It is out there, Lily, from many investigations." Bill frowned deeper as he helped her stand beside Loch. He could feel the shuddering of fear in her body.

Bill then stared at Lily's phone, not comprehending what he was reading. "Lily? Do you know this person?"

Lily was shaking her head. She had no idea who this person was but she wanted them. She didn't want to continue to live in fear. She had tried to give that over to God. Lily just didn't think that He was hearing her. She had begged for this to be over. Only the situation seemed to be getting much worse.

Loch wrapped her into his arms, his eyes on Bill, silently begging him to find out who it was. He had a deep-rooted fear that he was the one responsible for all this. He just didn't see how though.

"No, I don't, Bill. Make him stop. Or is it her?" Lily frowned even as she relaxed back against Loch. "Bill, why would someone be after Loch?"

Bill shrugged, seeing the attention that her words had garnered from the other men. He thought through her words, begging God to enlighten him and help him to understand.

"He took a photo that he shouldn't have? He refused to do a photo shoot?" Bill was grasping at the proverbial straw to understand what Lily was saying.

Loch was stunned at the suggestion that he might be the one responsible for what had happened. He had not even thought of that although he should have. He felt Lily's hands tighten on his.

"A photo shoot?" Loch shook his head. "I've refused some over the years but I'm not sure that I can remember them all. As to the question if I took something that I should have? I have thousands of photos. It would take weeks, if not months, to go over all of them. If we had a date range to work with, it would be more manageable."

"We understand that, Loch. It was just a suggestion." Bill shared a long look with Lily. "Lily?"

"Bill? I thought of that but decided that it wouldn't be the reason. Now you're saying that it could be? We could never prove that." Lily was distraught, her face pale with her fright.

"We know, Lily. We've been going back over the threats directed at you. Jason had a thought. He wants to look at the cases that you're working through or due to go to court with."

Lily stared at him before nodding. That could be it. Would one of her cases connect with Loch?

Chapter 37

Lily paced her office that evening, worried about Loch. Loch had been subdued when they came back to their home, and Lily had not known what to do or say. She had walked away at last, heading for her office. Sitting at her desk, she had thought through what she was facing in court, making a list that she could pass on to Jason or Bill.

Loch came looking for her, standing in the hallway to watch his bride. His heart broke for her. He wanted to be the one who had caused it all but he wasn't convinced that he was. He looked around, sensing someone near him but could not see anyone. He began to pray, petitioning his Heavenly Father for peace and resolution of what they were facing. Loch felt a peace begin to move through his heart, knowing that God was there with them. He was also aware that there were times when God's presence was felt in a deeper way. This was one of them he was sure.

Moving forward, Loch stood in Lily's path with his arms out to wrap around her. Lily jumped as he did so before her arms were around him. She was terrified, she had to admit, that she would be harmed but more terrified that Loch would be harmed. Luke seemed safe for now but that could change in a heartbeat, she had to acknowledge.

Content just to stand and be held, Lily looked up at Loch, frowning at the look on his face. Her mouth opened and closed. Loch in turn was studying her, his love for her evident on his face. His mouth too opened to speak but instead of speaking, he reached to kiss her.

"Lily? I love you. I am so glad that you are mine, no matter how it happened." Loch watched her face, seeing the emotions crossing her face.

"You do? I love you, Loch. I didn't ever expect us to be together." Lily tightened her hug on him.

"I do. I wish that I had been able to court you just as you deserve. That didn't happen. But know this. I am not walking away from you." Loch turned them to sit on the couch in the office. "We need to talk, Lily. We're still in danger. I am so afraid that I will lose you. And I don't know if my heart could take that."

Lily nestled down beside him, content to be beside the love of her life. Her thoughts were troubled and tumbling over one another. She frowned as she stared across the room, knowing that Loch was watching her.

"Lily? You're deep in thought."

"I am. I was thinking about what was said today. I need to go over my court cases. Somehow, there is a connection there between us that we're not aware of but someone has made it."

"I agree. Set it aside for the night, sweetheart. We'll take it up in the morning. I can't access my studio yet due to the investigation. You're on leave right now. Let's do something fun, just like we used to do."

They drifted off to sleep, confident that they would find the person responsible and soon. They didn't know that off-duty colleagues were around the house, keeping watch out for Lily and her fellow. They didn't know Loch, but were still worried about him. Lily had always gone above and beyond in helping anyone. They just wanted to repay her and this was one way that they could.

The next morning found Loch on his feet, standing and staring down at Lily who still slept. He walked away, heading for a shower and clean clothes before he walked to the front door and outside. He was startled to find an office stationed on the front porch.

"You're here?" Loch should not have been surprised.

"We have been all night, Loch. Lily is important to us and because she is, you are. You're part of our family now." The officer rose and stretched, heading for the steps. "Someone will be around all the time until this is over. Most times, you won't see us."

Loch nodded, his eyes closing for a moment. He felt a hand on his back and reached to wrap Lily close to him. She watched as the officer waved before he drove away.

"We're being taken care of, sweetheart." Lily leaned against Loch, drawing from his strength.

"We are, love. We are. Now, what can we do today that is fun?" Loch grinned at her. They needed that, he knew.

Late that afternoon, Lily and Loch walked back towards their home, hand in hand. They had managed to find something fun to do even though they had felt followed the whole time. They had just not seen anyone.

Lily dropped her phone to the kitchen table, staring at it. The text messages that she had been ignoring were vicious. She sighed. This was starting now. She forwarded them to both Jason and Bill, knowing that one of them would be in touch.

Loch wrapped her into his arms, his chin resting on her head. He had enjoyed that day, finding Lily even more fun to be with than as a teenager. However, there had been that feeling that they were still in danger and that something drastic was about to unfold. Loch didn't want that. He wanted to protect his lady and didn't know how he would do that.

"Lily? What are you thinking?" Loch waited patiently for Lily to think that question through.

"I'm not hiding any more, Loch. It's not accomplishing anything." Lily struggled to turn in his arms, looking up at him. "We need to make some plans. When can you go back to your studio?"

"Bill thought tomorrow. I'll grab my stuff that I need from the apartment. I'm not sure that I want to continue the studio there right now." Loch bit at his lip.

"We can do that. For now, let's spend some time in prayer. I know that we are praying separately but now that we're a couple, we need to do that together." Lily moved away from him, heading for the living room. “Loch, we need this. We need God’s protection more and more every day, at least until this is over.”

Loch nodded in agreement. He had come to the same conclusion. He simply sat and wrapped Lily into his arms, his head bowing as he waited in silence before God. Lily did the same. They had no idea how long they had sat like that but they rose at last, peace in their hearts and knowledge that God cared for and protected them. They were ready to make some plans to move forward to trap whoever it was.

Chapter 38

Jason stood in front of Lily an hour later. He had been on call when her text had arrived. He had read it, his face tightening with anger. Jason was fully aware and acknowledged that God had Lily's and Loch's lives in His hands and wanted only the best for them. He also was cognizant that what they wanted was not always God's plan and purpose for a person's life.

Lily stared up at Jason, not sure what to say. She knew that he was angry about the message but not at her or Loch. Loch was standing nearby, his focus on his phone but was still listening to Jason. He stopped at a photo that had just been sent to him. Turning, he simply handed Jason his phone.

Lily tilted Jason's hand to study the photo. That had been taken that day while they had been walking along the river. She drew in a deep breath, opened her mouth to speak, and then snapped it closed. Things were coming to a head, she decided, and didn't like that at all.

"Jason? This was taken when we were out today." Loch paced, his hand rubbing at his cheek. "I know that we're being followed. This was too close. We could have disappeared again."

"We know that, Loch. Someone was following you as well to watch out for you. Richard and his team are sharing that duty with off-duty officers. I don't know that they saw anything. Whoever is after you? They are watching you and watching the ones who are protecting you."

"We have a leak somewhere, Jason. But who?"

Jason was nodding. He had had that very conversation with Bill and Andrew that afternoon. They were at a loss, though, to know who the informer might be.

"Lily?" Loch waited for a moment, not sure how to express what he had to say.

Lily shrugged. She had no idea who might be that was leaking that information. She wanted that person. Even though she was not allowed to investigate, it would be what she would do. Jason studied her and nodded. He and the others knew that Lily would be looking for whoever it was. He just prayed that she was not hurt.

"I don't know, Loch. I truly don't." Lily turned back to her desk. Picking up a sheet of paper, she studied it before handing it off to Jason. "Here, Jason. These are the court cases that I have upcoming. The ones that I've starred? They are the ones more likely to have someone trying to discredit me."

Jason nodded, as he read through them. He frowned. Lily had starred ones that he had not thought of.

"Why these ones, Lily?"

"Because they involve higher ranking officials or people in town. If someone in their family was to be convicted of a serious crime, it would reflect back on them to their discredit. None of them have threatened me but I will find them watching me intently if I do see them." Lily began to pace once more. This time, she didn't allow either of the men to stop her. She just walked away from them, her thoughts troubled and black.

Loch reached for the paper, taking it from Jason before he read it. He began to nod before he reached for a different-coloured pen to begin to mark his own. Loch handed the paper back to Jason, his eyes on Lily.

Lily moved to stand between the two men, reading the names that Loch had marked. She began to nod. Loch had marked two or three names that she had. They would work on them. Her phone was out to take a photo of the paper. She would forward it to Emma and let her work on it.

Jason walked away at last, his thoughts on the name. He nodded at last. He would work on them and see what he could find. Jason also knew that Lily would be researching and investigating them even though she should not.

Loch turned from locking the door after Jason. He had stepped outside onto the front porch and had felt danger around him. He stepped quickly back into the house. Looking for Lily, Loch took the paper from her that she had printed from the information on her phone. With an arm around her, he led her back to the living room and shoved her to the couch before sitting beside her and wrapping her into his arms.

"We need to pray, love. This is where it gets so dangerous for us. I know that you want to be back and work but you're not ready to go yet." His head tilted as he watched the emotions flowing across her face. "You're having doubts about going back."

"I am." Lily was not surprised at his words. He was able to read her and always had been. "I don't know that I can go back. Right now, it's too dangerous for me to do so. I don't want to put anyone at risk." She settled back against him, her hand rubbing at the back of one of his. "I don't know if I want to go back now. There have been so many friends affected by danger. It wears you out."

"It does. I've heard the stories of them all, including those of Abe and his men and their friends. Richard told me about Don and his team from Oak City. That's a lot of people to go through things."

"It is but it happens." Lily sighed to herself. "We need to eat, Loch."

"And we will but for now? We pray." Loch bowed his head, his prayer echoing through the room.

Lily listened to his prayer, hearing the petition that he was raising to their Heavenly Father and the promises that were sprinkled throughout it. She leaned harder against Loch, not realizing that she was slipping away to sleep, feeling safe in his arms.

Loch felt Lily relaxing as he prayed. When he finished, his head tilted as he studied her. He nodded. She was asleep and there was no way that he was moving and disturbing her. The drapes had already been closed for the night and soft lighting filled the room.

Digging out his phone as it vibrated, Loch frowned at the number. He pulled up the text message that Frankie Brennan had sent and then pulled up the email. He read through it, frowning as he did so. Loch nodded and then forwarded the email to both Jason and Bill. Frankie had some information that they needed and needed then.

Chapter 39

Lily walked through the downtown area the next morning. She was on a search but she was also putting herself out there as a target. Loch was involved in deciding what he wanted to do about his apartment and had told her to go find something to do or someone to have coffee with a friend. He had kissed her as he sent her on her way, reluctant to do so when he was not with her.

Entering the bookstore run by a friend, Lily wandered the aisles, pulling a book off the shelf here and there, reading the synopsis on the back, and then setting it back in its place. She paused at the coffee area that Suzanne had set up, poured herself a coffee, and then headed for Suzanne's office.

Suzanne looked up as she heard Lily's footsteps and sat back in her chair, waiting for her friend to speak. She was patient, knowing that Lily was troubled and would speak when she could.

"Suzanne? Have you heard any rumours about Loch or myself?" Lily knew that her friend would be honest with her.

"No, I haven't, Lily. I think that if there are rumours out there, they are not being repeated to your friends or fellow officers. That's being done to protect you." Suzanne rubbed at her temple, the headache developing more and more. "I wish someone would. Then, you could find the person and be done with this."

"I know. That's what I want. I want to go on with my life. Loch loves me and I love him. Yet, we feel that the danger is just so close to us that we don't know where to turn or what to do. And before you ask, we have spoken with Silas and I have sought out Madigan, Phoebe, and Cora."

"That's good. You need that support." Suzanne sat forward, leaning her elbows on the desk. "You have names."

"We do." Lily pulled out her phone, found the document and then handed her phone to Suzanne. "The ones that are starred? Those are the ones who we suspect."

Suzanne nodded, reading through the names. She looked up at Lily, finding Lily watching her intently.

"Can I have a copy of this?" At Lily's nod, she forwarded the list to her own phone. "Why these ones, Lily?"

Lily shrugged. She had no idea why she had picked those names but she acknowledged that God had been behind it. He was bringing their adventure to a close and giving her the information that she needed to do so. They just had to determine who it really was and bring them to justice.

"I want whoever this is." Lily rose and began to pace, not sure what to say. "This is hurting us in a way that they shouldn't. I know. God is in control and He is working this out for His glory. I just want it over."

"That's understandable, Lily. Now, how do we find out which one this is? They're business owners. I can work it from that way." Suzanne was already trying to determine a way to do that.

"Take care, Suzanne. These people are brutal. They won't hesitate to harm or even kill anyone who gets in their way." Lily sat back down, burying her head in her hands. "I am so scared, Suzanne. I don't want anyone hurt because of me. And that's my fear."

"It's natural to fear that, Lily. We're praying for you and Loch." Suzanne grinned at her. "You and Loch were always meant to be. We all could see that when we were teens. God brought him back into your life." She looked down for a moment. "Lily? Where do you go now with your work?" Her voice was hesitant as she asked that.

"I don't know, Suzanne. I'm not sure any more that I want to be a police officer. I'm jumping at any little noise and looking around. I can't work like that. I am praying it through as is Loch. Luke likely is too." She looked up. "You're asking that for a reason."

"I am. I am looking for someone to come in as a partner and your name keeps coming up as I pray about it. Think about it. Pray about it. Talk with Loch." Suzanne rose as Lily stood. "No pressure, my friend. Just pray it through."

"I will." Lily reached to hug her friend. "Thank you. This may help take my mind off what I am going through. I just don't want to bring any danger to you." She looked around as she heard a throat clear and then was in Loch's arms. "Loch? How did you know?"

"Some little birdie told me where to find you. Are you ready to go out for lunch?" Loch grinned at Suzanne.

"I am. Thank you, Suzanne. I'll let you know my decision soon." Lily walked away, her hand tight in Loch's grip, leaving Suzanne praying for her friends.

"What was that all about?" Loch tugged her towards their favourite diner.

"Suzanne offered me a partnership in the book shop." Lily bit at her lip, her eyes on the man standing near the diner. She had bad vibes from him and didn't want to walk past him.

"She did? Yes, I could see that. You would do well there. I know we're praying through what you want to do." Loch passed the man, frowning as he did so. The man seemed familiar to him but he shrugged. There were just too many people that he felt that way about.

Lily slid into a booth, Loch beside her. They nodded at the server before Loch reached for her hand.

"Lily? Are you sure about leaving the force?" Loch knew how her heart was hurting at that decision.

Lily shrugged. She wasn't sure at all about leaving but she was also not sure about staying. She didn't have the peace that she needed at the moment to show her what decision to make.

"I don't know, Loch." She stared around the diner, focusing on a trio of men who sat nearby. She frowned before her phone was out and a photo taken of them. Her finger was in the air as she forwarded the photo to Bill. “Those three men? They were there when I was beaten. I’m sure of it. I just don’t know what they want from us.”

“And they want something. I don’t either.” Loch was lost in thought, moving his arms automatically as his meal was set in front of him. “Lily? Can you determine who they are?”

“I can. We’ll head for the department once we’re done our meal. I need to head that way any way to see what is on my desk and what I need to deal with. That way, we can talk to either Jason or Bill about them.”

Chapter 40

Lily walked through the department, stopping to greet her fellow officers and the civilian employees. She unlocked her office door and flipped on the lights as she entered. Loch followed to stand and watch her as she stood at her desk.

"What do you need to do first, love?" Loch grinned at her as she shook her finger at him.

"I need to go through all this. You'll be bored." Lily sat at her desk and began to sort through what sat on it.

"No, it's okay. I have some stuff that I can do." Loch began to work away on his phone, glancing up once in a while to watch his bride. He was very worried about her. Things were coming to a head, he decided, but he didn't know how to resolve it.

Bill walked through the building an hour later, pausing in surprise as he saw Lily's door open. He stood where he could watch her, seeing the concentration on her face. He had just come from meeting a street person who had handed over information to him. Bill knew that he needed to talk with Lily. He just didn't know how to and that had never been a problem for him. He walked on by to find Andrew and spent almost an hour discussing the case. Bill rose at last, heading back to Lily's office, finding her still engrossed in her work. Loch looked up this time and nodded at Bill before he rose and headed out of the office.

"Bill? What have you found?"

"Someone has come forward with information about you two and what you are facing. I need to work through it and then talk with you two. I'll be around this evening." Bill watched Lily. "How is she?"

"She's hurting, Bill. She's not sure if she wants to continue working as an officer." Loch rubbed at his face, knowing that being an officer had been all that Lily had wanted to do and it was a strong part of her personality.

"She will have those doubts. I did. Cora and I prayed and talked it through. It was hard to do, knowing that I could be putting everyone at risk. Andrew had the same decision to make." Bill watched as Lily looked up and then rose to come out to stand beside Loch, having his arm wrapped around her.

"Bill? You have news?" Lily read Bill correctly.

"I do, Lily. Someone came forward with some information. I'll work it through and then come see you and Loch tonight." Bill walked away, leaving Loch to wrap Lily tighter into his arms.

"Let's head home, Lily, if you're ready to do so." Loch walked her back into her office. "I need to stop at the studio for a few moments if we can."

"That's not a problem, Loch." Lily tidied away what she had been working on and then locked her door. "What are you up to?"

Loch shrugged, a grin on his face. Stopping at the studio, Loch walked through it, knowing that he wanted to move it to another building. There was a building that he had inherited near the edge of town. He was making plans to move his studio to there.

“Loch? What are your thoughts?” Lily wrapped her arms around him, stopping him in his tracks.

“That I want to move the studio. There’s a building near the edge of town that would be better suited to it. I set it up here just because of the apartment. It was convenient at the time.” Loch studied Lily’s face, seeing her understanding on her face.

“The Wallis building? That would work. I had forgotten about it. How be we stop by there? It’s empty, isn’t it?” Lily turned to tug him from the studio, waiting as the door was locked and Loch reached for her hand.

“We can. I’m not sure we’re safe doing that.” Loch turned from the steering wheel that he sat in front of to study her.

“Luke can come.” Lily looked up from her phone. “And Timothy and Stephen will come.” Timothy and Stephen were the two men on Richard’s security team. Timothy said that he was expecting this.”

“Timothy would. He has always thought ahead of everyone else.” Loch drove off, watching as a car pulled out from the curb and followed them. “We have a shadow, Lily.”

Lily twisted in her seat, a hand holding her seatbelt away from her body for a moment. The car was not close enough for her to see the license plate number. She called in a description of it, knowing that it was not a patrol vehicle.

Walking through the building, Loch knew that he was making the right decision. This would work much better than the other building. Lily stood in the centre of what would be a reception area and looked around as well. She nodded. This was so much better.

"Lily? What do you think?" Loch approached her and wrapped her in a hug, kissing her as he did so.

"I like this, Loch. This will work out better for you. There is a lot more light here."

"There is." Loch looked past her as the door opened. "Timothy?"

"Loch?" Timothy grinned as he mimicked his tone of voice. "Stephen's outside as is Luke."

"I figured as much. I'll need you to go over this building and set up security for me. And I'll need to find someone to set it up the way that I want."

"We can do that. I know of a carpenter who will work with you. Adam." Timothy grinned at Loch.

"Adam? Of course, he'll work with me. I'm in no rush. Now, what about that car that followed us?"

"That car? It went on past the street. Naomi and Silver are following it. Richard is coordinating us from the office. Did you really think that we would just drop it?" Timothy's voice had grown stern.

"No, I didn't. I just didn't know if the car had stopped here or left." Loch's arms tightened around Lily.

“They’re following you closely, Loch. Lily, you know what that means.” Timothy stood in front of the door, arms crossed across his chest.

“I know, Timothy. I know. We’re not getting all the threats and packages that others did.” Lily blinked. “I think that someone on the force is involved and that someone is close to me. I just don’t know who or how to find it out.” She looked up at Loch. “I have asked Jason and Bill to investigate that.”

Chapter 41

Two weeks later, Lily was back at her desk, working through the investigations that crossed it. She was saddened that she no longer had the spark and joy that she had felt before in helping solve the investigations. She knew that Bill and Andrew were watching her, waiting for her to come to them. Lily didn't. She wasn't ready to make that decision even though she and Loch were praying it through. She had only wanted to be a police officer but was now at a crossroads in her life and a decision needed to be made.

On her feet, Lily walked towards Jason's office, a file in her hands. She waited for him to finish his phone call before he waved her into his office. Lily sat after dropping the file on his desk.

"What is this, Lily?"

"I don't know, Jason, but it involves Loch and myself. How did that come to me?" Lily was shaken at what she had read.

Jason read through it, a sternness crossing his face. This was a direct threat at Lily and Loch.

"Lily? This is a threat towards you and Loch!"

"I know, Jason. I know. I know that name. He's one of the workers in the men's shelters. How do we do this?" Lily was distraught at that. She had worked with him in the past.

"We keep you away from him at all times. If a call comes in from that area, one of the others responds. We also need to talk with Bill."

"Only Bill and Cora are away for a few days." Lily blew out a breath. "We need to find Loch. Only I don't have my car. He dropped me off today."

Jason was on his feet, taking a photo of the man's picture, and then pointing towards the door. There was no conversation between the two detectives as they travelled towards Loch's new studio that was under construction.

Lily was out of Jason's car and running for the studio, shoving open the door and searching for Loch. He was nowhere to be found. Lily stood in the centre of what could be his workroom and rubbed at her temple. Loch should have been here as should Adam.

Jason walked through the building and then around the outside of it. Both Loch's and Adam's trucks were there but the men didn't seem to be around. He cupped his hands around his face as he stared into their vehicles. No one was in them.

Turning as he heard footsteps on the gravel driveway, he frowned at Adam.

"Adam? Where were you?"

"Out back. Loch was wanting to see what he could develop out there for an outside studio. He's heading into the building. What are you doing here?" Adam planted his feet, not moving as Jason pointed back at the building.

"We need to speak with both Loch and Lily. There has been a development that will affect you working for him."

"I'm not walking away from him, Jason. He needs to have this done and he is a friend." Adam walked back towards the building, Jason pacing beside him.

Loch looked around as the two men entered the building. He had been able to determine why Lily was there and that bothered him. He had had no contact with that man and couldn't understand the threats that Lily had informed him of.

"Jason?" Loch's anger laced his voice. "How do you find and arrest this man?"

"We're working on it, Loch. He'll be arrested today. In the mean while, we need to keep you and Lily safe. Adam? Can you leave what you're doing today?"

"I can, Jason. Loch, call me when you're able to pick back up the work. I'll work on plans for the outside for you." Adam walked away, troubled about his friends.

Lily kept her eyes locked on Jason's face, seeing the struggle that he was going through. She understood it completely. She had been there in the past.

"Lily? We need to put you and Loch somewhere for the day and overnight. We're working on the arrest warrant but until then, you need to be out of sight." Jason was stern with Lily, knowing that he had to be.

Lily would not willingly to go along with him, that much he knew.

"I get that, Jason. Where are we heading?" Lily reached for Loch's hand, knowing that their freedom for the day had just walked away.

"We take you home to pack a bag for each of you. Then, we'll stick you away somewhere. Richard is weighing."

Lily snorted. She knew right well that Richard would weigh in. It's what he did.

"He'll have a place for us, I know that. Let's get this show on the road, then." Lily watched as an officer took Loch's keys to lock up the building and then drive Loch's car to their home.

Lily wandered the living room of the house that Richard had brought them to. Richard was well aware of what to watch for. She just hadn't wanted it to come to that. She could hear Loch as he spoke with Andrew, asking the questions that she knew he wanted answers to. Only those were not forthcoming at this time.

Richard studied his friend, seeing the stress that lined Lily's face. He was worried about her.

"Lily? What about this man?" Richard's question drew her attention.

Lily shrugged. She had no idea why he would threaten her and Loch.

"I don't know, Richard. You know the man. Have you ever sensed anything evil about him?" Lily was now doubting how she had read him.

“I think so. Raleigh mentioned that just a couple of weeks ago. She said that she didn’t feel comfortable around him, that there was an evilness about him.” Richard sighed. “She’s right. He’s changed over the past few years.”

“He was hiding who he was. He’s not from this town so we had no idea that he was not who he seemed to be.” Lily bit at her lip. “Jason is looking into him and planning on arresting him today. I want to know who he was working for.”

“We all do. This needs to end for you and Loch.” Richard reached to hug his friend before he walked away to the outside, knowing that his emotions were on edge for his friend.

Chapter 42

That night, Lily's head raised from the pillow she had it on. She had curled up in one of the rooms, a light blanket over her. She had been waiting for something to happen. Reaching for her weapon, Lily was on her feet, heading for the main portion of the house. Loch's hand landed on her back as she crept forward, bringing comfort to her and also an awareness that he could be hurt, depending on what she found.

Stopping in the hallway before she reached the living room, Lily waited, barely seeming to breathe. Loch's hand lay heavy on her back. He didn't want to break contact with her at any point but knew that if he had to, he would step back and let her do what she needed to do.

A sound from the front door had Lily turning that way although she did not move from where she had stopped in the darkness. She frowned at the sound. Someone had entered the house or more than one person. Lily tilted her head even more. One person was not steady on their feet. She prayed for that person, worried that it was either Stephen or Timothy who had volunteered to work overnight.

The sound of a body hitting the floor made her jump. She felt Loch's hand clutch at her back. Not being really familiar with the house had its disadvantages. She didn't know where to go to escape.

Loch grew increasingly worried. He too had heard the sound of a body hitting the floor and he prayed for whoever it was.

The men stood in the living room area, Stephen on the floor at their feet. He was still, blood trickling from his forehead where a revolver butt had landed. Timothy had not been close enough to help his friend and team mate but had faded into the trees, his phone out to call for assistance. He crept closer to the house, finding a spot near the front door yet hidden behind shrubs where he could hear what was happening. His heart sank as he realized that Stephen was down and there was nothing that he could do to help him. His phone was out as he sent a text off to Richard, knowing that Richard would find Naomi and Silver and head his way.

The man who was the leader of the three men paced the living room. He didn't like that they had had to take down a man. That had not been in the plan. He had ensured that Stephen was only knocked out and not killed. They were there for Lily and Loch.

Lily backed away from the door, forcing Loch to move back silently. She shoved him into a bedroom and shut the door behind her, her eyes searching in the dark. She could not help whichever man it was who was on the floor. She frowned at Loch as he stood in front of her, hands on her shoulders and with his eyebrows raised in question.

"The window, Loch. Let's see if we can get out that way." Lily tucked her weapon into her waistband and was across the room, unlocking the window and sliding it to one side.

Loch reached to help her, the screen quietly lifted from its track and dropped to the ground. He was through the window, landing quietly on his feet, and then reaching for his bride. He feared for her. Loch wanted to live the rest of his life with the lady whom he loved. Only that didn't seem to be likely.

They crept away from the house, heading for the detached garage, and then around it towards the neighbours yard. Creeping through it, Lily paused and reached for her weapon before her hand was withdrawn from it and she was reaching for Loch's hand. She ran towards the dark figure that was waiting for them, beckoning them forward.

Jason herded Loch and Lily away from the house and towards a vehicle. He shoved them inside before standing with his back to the door. He watched as forms appeared in front of him.

"Timothy?" His voice was low. "What happened?"

"Three men moved in on Timothy before he could escape. He's down and in the house. Lily and Loch. Managed to escape from a window and headed this way." Timothy was very worried about his friend. "We need to get in there."

"And we will. Stay here." Jason moved away with the officer who had appeared as well behind Timothy.

Timothy watched closely but didn't hear the men who had approached him. He was in a chokehold before he realized what was going and dragged away from the car. The car door flew open and Lily and Loch were pulled from the vehicle and gags slapped on their faces. They too were dragged from the area, their steps tracking in Timothy's path. The three were shoved into a van and driven away. Loch's hand found Lily's and gripped it tightly. He watched where they were being driven to. He could feel her anger and saw that Timothy was angry as well.

The men dropped out of the vehicle as it stopped in an industrial building, the large overhead door dropping down behind them. The three captives sat quietly, Lily and Timothy running scenarios as to how they could get away.

Lily's hand tore away her gag and then did the same for Loch's. She twisted and turned on her seat, trying to keep track of the men. She knew that Timothy was doing the same.

"Timothy? Are you okay?" Lily's voice was low.

"I am. You two are?" Timothy drew in a deep breath as she nodded. "Stephen? Did you see him?"

"No, but I heard a body hit the floor. It must have been him." Lily dropped to the floor and reached for the door handle. "They're not around, Timothy, and we're close to the door. They didn't take our weapons."

"No, and that's odd." Timothy was out of the van and at the door, his hand reaching for the knob. Surprise coloured his face as it turned and opened for him. Lily and Loch were through it right behind him, running for the edge of the property and finding a spot in the fence that they could crawl through. Lily took the lead with Loch behind her. Timothy ran behind Loch, watchful for anyone who was following them.

The men stared in shock at the open van door and then the open side door of the building. They were sure that the three would not be able to escape. Yet, that had been exactly what had happened. They searched both inside and outside the building, not finding them. They stared at each other, dumbstruck at the events. None of them wanted to face their employer. They crept away to their vehicles and drove off. They just kept driving, leaving behind whatever it was that they had left in their apartments.

Lily slid to a stop eventually, her breathing heavy. Loch stood behind her with a hand on her back, his head turning as he looked around. Timothy moved past them, looking for a way out of the area before he was back in short order, silently beckoning for them to follow him. They walked silently through the quiet streets, heading for the downtown area. A vehicle slowly approached them, causing them to move to the shadows of the trees before Timothy gave an exclamation and drew Lily and Loch towards the car. They were inside and the car driving away, Richard sharing a look with Timothy. The tracking device that Timothy was wearing had paid off and Richard had found them.

Chapter 43

Jason stood in the living room of the house. The police officers had been able to move in quietly without the men hearing them. Shock had coloured the men's faces as they saw the officers waiting for them. Handcuffs were quietly clicked around their wrists before they were led from the house and shoved into patrol cars.

He himself had helped Stephen to his feet, watching carefully as that man was assessed by the paramedics. Stephen shrugged off their requests to be seen at the hospital. He had taken harder hits than that, he told them. He would go if he felt that he had to. He turned to Jason who simply pointed to the door.

Once seated in Jason's car, Stephen opened his mouth and then closed it. He had been told that Timothy, Lily, and Loch had disappeared. No one had seen anything but the three had disappeared from Jason's car. That worried him more than he wanted to admit. Bill had been around and then headed out to search as well.

Stephen pulled out his phone, grumbling at its incessant vibrating. He read the text and then read it again.

"Richard has them, Jason. He's heading for the department with them." Stephen pocketed his phone after responding to the text. "They're okay."

"He has them. Okay." Jason pulled out his phone and sent a quick message to Bill and then to dispatch before he headed for the department. He almost ran for the back door, Stephen following him closely. He dropped his jacket in his office and then searched for Bill.

“Bill?” Jason slid to a stop in front of him, Stephen at his side.

“They’re giving their statements right now, Jason. Then, we’ll talk with them. Richard and Timothy are in the conference room. Head that way.” Bill walked away, fatigue weighing him down. He had not been home yet, having been called back in as he arrived home.

Jason headed for the break room, pouring coffee for himself and Stephen. Then he directed Stephen towards the conference room, finding Richard and the two ladies waiting for them.

“Richard?” Jason set his coffee mug on the table before he turned to the other man.

“We found them walking this way. They didn’t say anything.” Richard was concerned about Stephen. “Stephen? Timothy said that you were hurt.”

“Yeah. I was knocked out. I’m fine.” Stephen slumped into a chair, his head cradled in his hands. His team members exchanged looks, knowing that Stephen would not relax until he knew that the three who had disappeared were fine.

The door opened quietly as Timothy slipped into the room. He approached Stephen, quiet words exchanged between the two men.

Lily waited in the hallway for Loch to appear. He wrapped her in his arms, her tears wetting his shirt. He dropped a kiss on the top of her head, knowing how she was struggling with what had happened.

"Okay, sweetheart?" Loch kept his voice low, standing out of the way of the officers passing by them.

"I am, Loch. And you?" Lily looked up at him, tear tracks on her cheeks.

"I am. I think this is going to end it, Lily. Here, where can you wash off your tears? Then, we'll find the others and see where we stand."

Lily nodded and headed for the washroom. She soaked paper towels in as hot of water as she could, staring at her image in the mirror. This is it, she decided. There had to be an answer that would be available. She returned to where Loch was waiting, walking back into his arms and hugging him in return.

Jason looked around as the door to the conference room opened and Lily and Loch appeared. He hesitated before he approached them, his head tilting to study them.

"Lily?" Jason's voice was quiet and controlled. He didn't let his worry and anger come through.

"I'm okay, Jason. So is Loch and Timothy." She told him what had happened, leaving him puzzled.

"Lily? I'm going to ask you a question. Think about it before you answer. And then, Loch? Timothy? I want your response as well." He waited for all three of them to nod. "Lily? The men who took you from Jason's car and then left you in the building?

Did they seem to mean you harm? Or did they take you to protect you?"

Lily nodded at his words. She had been thinking the same thing.

"I think I am not sure what they wanted. They didn't say a word. It was just so bizarre. We were gagged and then dragged to a van. The van was driven inside a building and then they left us alone. We were able to get away but shouldn't have." Lily paused to think through what had happened. "I would suspect that they are the ones who have been after us. Driving us inside a building like that would have made them think that we could not escape. They just weren't very smart."

"No, they weren't smart." Loch paced away from his bride and then around the room. He was puzzled about what happened. "They kidnapped us and then didn't take us anywhere, really, other than across town. They didn't think that we would escape. God provided that opportunity for us. Are they still in town or have they run?"

"I would think that they likely have run." Jason rubbed at his cheek. He was exhausted but couldn't leave to go home. Not yet.

"Loch, that name that we came to last night?" Lily turned to her groom, finding him nodding. "He works overnight in his office. He always has. Let's go face him." Lily strode away, stopping in her office to retrieve an extra holster. She fastened it to her belt and dropped her weapon in it before she grabbed a sweatshirt that she had in the office and pulled it over her head. She noted that someone had provided a sweatshirt for Loch and knew that she would find that man and thank him.

Jason's hand stopped her in her tracks.

"Lily? Are you sure about this?"

"I am. Bill has gone to get the warrants that we need." Lily looked around Jason to see Bill there. "We're ready, Bill?"

"We are. Let's go find this man, Lily, and then get you two home." Bill walked away with Lily, Loch walking beside Jason. He would not stay in the station. He wanted to be there and face the man who had caused all their trouble.

Chapter 44

Lily stood in front of a store near the police department, her eyes intent on the light that was showing inside. She waited patiently as Bill and his team approached the door and hammered at it. Her eyes were lifted to the man who appeared, a tall and thin older man. Lily could tell that he was protesting the invasion that night. She sighed as he began to struggle with the officers, ending up on the sidewalk and with handcuffs binding his hands behind his back.

Bill dragged him to his feet, his hand tight on the man's upper arm. He shoved him forward and stopped in front of Lily. He knew that she wanted answers and he was willing to let her have her say.

"Ward Blouin. Of course, it's you." Lily spat out her words. He had always seemed so upright in his life and profession of jeweler. There had been rumours about him smuggling over the years but nothing had been proven. "What did Loch and I ever do to you?"

"You lived." Blouin spat at her, missing her as she stepped to one side. "You weren't supposed to live." He almost began to foam at the mouth, his anger was that great. "That bus accident? You two were supposed to be on it and die. Only you weren't. It's your fault that I couldn't leave town. I had all this money socked away but had to spend it on rehab for my son. You were always the golden kids, not doing anything wrong. Everyone looked down on my son and he blamed you two for that."

"Your son? Who is your son?" Loch spoke for both of them.

"Johnny Ward."

Lily blinked at Blouin's words. They had no idea that Blouin and Ward were related. Ward had not been a popular kid, bullying others. Loch knew that he and Luke had stepped in many times to protect others and stop his abuse.

"Your son? And he was injured in that accident? You caused your son to be crippled and blamed others. You were trying to kill him." Lily's voice held her confidence in that. "We had nothing to do with him or you. Your smuggling? It was always rumoured but no one had ever proven it. Not until now. The investigators will look thoroughly into your business. And I am sorry that you feel we did this to you. You did it to yourself. And now you will face justice not only from this but from God." Lily turned and walked away, a slump to her shoulders.

Loch had his arm around her, looking up in surprise as he saw Luke there in front of them. Richard had called Luke, simply asking him to come.

Lily looked up and then ran for her brother, finding him sweeping her into a big brother hug. She wept against him, the stress and strain of the past few weeks more than she could handle. Luke felt her slumping and gathered her into his arms, heading for the department building. Loch kept pace with her, not seeing the officers that surrounded them.

Lily struggled out of her brother's arms as he approached the steps to the building. She searched for

Loch, almost running to him. He shared a look with Luke who simply nodded. Lily turned at last and headed into the building, Loch and Luke on either side of her.

Bill found her a few hours later. She was seated at her desk, deep in work. Loch was settled into a chair, seemingly asleep. Luke was also asleep, confident that his sister was safe at last. Lily looked up and then rose, approaching Bill.

"Bill? Is it over?" Lily could barely speak, wanting it over but not sure that it was.

"It is, Lily. He was the only one. I feel sorry for his wife. I've spoken with her. She's leaving town now that she has the freedom to do so."

"A battered woman. I pray that she finds help." Lily sighed, leaning against the wall.

"She is. I've given her some resources that she can look in to. It bothers me that it could get to this point. I would never have known that Ward was his son."

"He's not his wife's son. He was the product of one of his affairs. His wife not likely could say anything or protest. That's how I'm reading her."

"No, she was beaten down in many ways." Bill agreed with Lily.

Loch had awakened and had come to stand behind Lily. Bill shared a look with him and then nodded before moving away. He still had work to do that night before he could head for home. The interrogation would take place in the morning.

Loch wrapped Lily in his arms, knowing that their adventure was over except for wrapping it up. They would need to face their antagonist in court at some point. But for now, they could start their life together. God had protected them and brought them through what they faced. They might never know why but they didn't need to. They were content with that.

Bill stared at the floor for a moment, not sure how to express what he needed to say. He looked up to find Luke standing in the doorway.

"Loch? It was Blouin who stabbed you that night. He thought that you would be blamed for the murder. It was part of his plot to discredit Lily, making it seem that she had not done a thorough investigation. The men who kidnapped you were his men. He was behind everything."

"Our marriage? Was he responsible?" Loch could barely get out the words.

"He was, Loch. I'm sorry, Lily, that it happened the way it did but I'm not sorry that you and Loch are married. You are two parts of a whole. He thought to discredit Lily in an investigation. The Hudson one, Lily. That was his cousin. Blouin's thoughts were that if he discredited you, the investigation would get thrown out."

"His mind has warped, as they say. He's living in a world where reality no longer exists." Lily leaned back against Loch once more, finding comfort in his hold. She shared a look with Luke. "I think that he's always been like that. We just didn't understand."

"No, we didn't understand and we should have. He has affected many lives in this town. We'll sort through it all and bring the charges that we need to. Go home, you three. It's going to be a rough few days as you come to terms with what has happened." Bill walked away, his heart heavy for his friends but thankful that God had protected them and led them to the one responsible.

Epilogue

Lily turned as she heard footsteps behind her. Loch swept her into his arms, kissing her thoroughly. It was a year after Blouin had been arrested. They had faced him in court, their testimony helping to send him away for many years. Their love had grown over the months. Both had admitted that they had had a crush on each other during their teens but had not acted on it.

Lily looked up at the tall, good-looking man who loved her so deeply. She was thankful every day that God had brought back into her life.

"Ready to leave for our trip, sweetheart?" Loch stared down at the beautiful face looking up at him.

"I am. I am so thankful that we have that cabin tucked away up north. We need that. The court cases took a lot from us. I wonder what happened to the men he had hired."

"I imagine that they left town after we disappeared. I still think that someone else was involved." Loch had been adamant about that.

"I know but I think that we found everyone." Lily moved away from him, a frown on her face. She had to admit that she had the same feeling.

"Let's get on the road, then, sweetheart." Loch reached to hug her again, thankful that she was in his life.

“I need to talk to you first, Loch.” Lily moved restlessly in his arms. “I’ve decided not to continue as an officer. I was approached by the woman’s shelter.”

“You were? That doesn’t surprise me. You’re taking over as the director?”

Lily nodded.

“I’m praying that way. That just happened this morning or I would have talked to you.”

“I know. I think that you will do well in that position. Your experience will help. And you have a long list of resources that will step in as well.”

“I do.” Lily was saddened that she was giving up what had been her dream job, but she felt the nudge from God to move on. “Loch? Would we have been married if you had not returned to town?”

“I think so, Lily. I came back to this town because you were here. I was trying to gather up the courage to approach you and ask you out when that murder happened.”

“That murder. Do you know that it was Blouin who did that? He was trying to frame you for that.”

“I wondered at that. And then he had me stabbed, right?” Lily’s nod confirmed that. “He really is a sick sad man.”

“He is. That’s what sin does to you.” Lily hugged Loch again before they kissed. “I am so thankful that we have faith. God was there for us each step of the way.”

"He was, sweetheart. He was. He brought the love of my life through a dangerous adventure. Now, we're off on a new adventure and a new chapter in our lives." Loch was content to stand and hold the lady who loved him and who he loved in return. God indeed had been gracious and protected them both.

They both realized that over the course of the adventure that they had not spoken much of their love for one another, too concerned with finding out who was responsible. They had rectified that, speaking much of their love and showing it in the little things that made up their daily life.

Dear Readers:

Thank you for picking up the story of Lily and her fellow, Loch. Lily was prominent in other stories from Elmton but was patiently waiting for her story to be told. This is it.

Once again, the characters just took over the story and wrote it themselves. I was only along as the fingers who typed it. Throughout their adventure, they knew that God was in control and had a purpose for what they were facing. Their adventure drove them closer to God and closer to one another.

That is what happens when we wait for God's leading. He directs us and guides us along the path that He had already laid out for us.

Many characters have walked into the story. Abe and Emma and his team are *His Guardians*. Adam and that group of friends are *His Warriors*. Silas and Madigan are *Strong Courage*. Bill and Cora is *Hidden in the Hollow*. Andrew and Phoebe is *The Potter's Hands*.

May God bless each one of you as you walk through life hand in hand with Him. Wait on Him. His plans sometimes take time to come to fruition. That's when we need to trust Him.

Ronna

www.ingramcontent.com/pod-product-compliance
Lightning Source LLC
Chambersburg PA
CBHW070345200726
48294CB00003B/790

9781998821334